The New Land is a magical  ıe
describes the fictional land ıe
setting is real. The descriŗ ıd
mountains are expertly paiı ıe
beginning of the novel.

The New Land would be ____ ___ ____ __ ___tasy novels
like Harry Potter and other novels about magical powers. The
Merlin and King Arthur references in the novel would also
appeal to fans of medieval fantasy. The book would be great
for readers of The Lord of the Rings trilogy or other Tolkien-
esque novels about journeys. Though the novel may appeal
most to young adult readers, The New Land can appeal to
readers of all ages.

Daisy Bourne has written a book that will have readers
clamoring [SIC] for more. The New Land will have readers
eager to return to Avalon

--Pacific Book Review

*'The New Land' was chosen as one of Pacific Book Review's
five Books of the Month in January 2017.*

Tales of King Arthur and Merlin will probably always be told
and re-told for new generations, but it's up to the author to
keep the stories fresh. This particular presentation does just
that for the younger audience.

Bourne does an admirable job of building this into a
believable new world and populating it with an assortment
of interesting characters.

--US Review of Books

THE NEW LAND

Book One
in
The Tales of Avalon
Series

BY DAISY BOURNE

For Kye and Ruby-Jo,
our wonderful grandchildren

Published 2017, in Great Britain,

Text Copyright © Daisy Bourne 2017

British Cataloguing Publication data:
A catalogue record of this book is available from
the British Library

This book is also available as an ebook.

CONTENTS

CHARACTERS

List of main characters, in alphabetical order.

Ajax: green dragon; husband of Blitzen

Alexander: the blacksmith's son (usually referred to as Alex); brother of Andrew; friend of Edward.

Alfred: an elf.

Allarond: King of the Elves

Andrew: the blacksmith's son; brother of Alexander; friend of Edward.

Arthur: King of Avalon (once King of Briton); husband of Gilda the witch; father of Edward-Arthur and Rosalie.

Azgoose: a witch who can create clouds of goo

Bizzbuzz: a wizard who specialises in making honey

Blitzen: blue Dragon; wife of Ajax

Bramble Family:

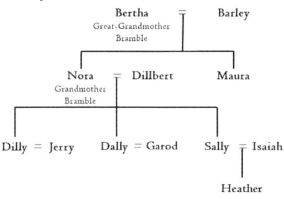

Comet: Merlin's white stallion

Connie: the baker's daughter

Daisy: the last of the Brewins

Derrick: Prince of Twydell; son of King Frederrick and Queen Elise

Edward-Arthur: illegitimate son of King Arthur (usually referred to simply as Edward)

Elise: wife/consort of King Frederrick of Twydell (given the title of queen at the time of marriage)

Elvira: Queen of the Witches in Briton and in Avalon; many of her witches migrated to Avalon

Esmerelda: Queen of the Witches (after Elvira); daughter of Elvira

Farainne: wife/consort of Allarond, King of the Elves (given the title of queen at the time of marriage)

Frederrick: King of Twydell

Gilda: one of the first witches to migrate to Avalon; she later married King Arthur; mother of Rosalie

Greatog: former leader of the giants; killed in an earlier battle with the Trajaens; father of Zog

Helen-Joy: a soothsayer

Jeanette: Princess of Twydell; daughter of King Frederrick and Queen Elise

Jeffrey: King of Kerner

Jonathan: a young warlock who specialises in plants (herbologist); son of the wizard Yzor and a half-witch

Lennox: last of the unicorns of Briton

Maud: Queen of the Fairies; married to Selogon

Merlin: powerful wizard who organised the migration to Avalon; advisor to King Arthur

Rabbart lll: King of Barrmin

Rosalie: daughter of King Arthur and Gilda the witch

Selogon: husband/consort of Maud, Queen of the Fairies

Shirley-Poppy: wife/consort of Jeffrey, King of Kerner (given the title of queen at the time of marriage)

Steven: Prince of Kerner; son of King Jeffrey and Queen Shirley-Poppy

Tannitus: powerful wizard; father of Tannus

Tannus: powerful young warlock; son of Tannitus

Willy the Wood Wizard: wizard who can talk to trees

Wormald the Wise: wise old wizard

Yzor: a wizard who specialises in plants (herbologist); father of Jonathan

Zog: leader of the giants; son of Greatog

MAP

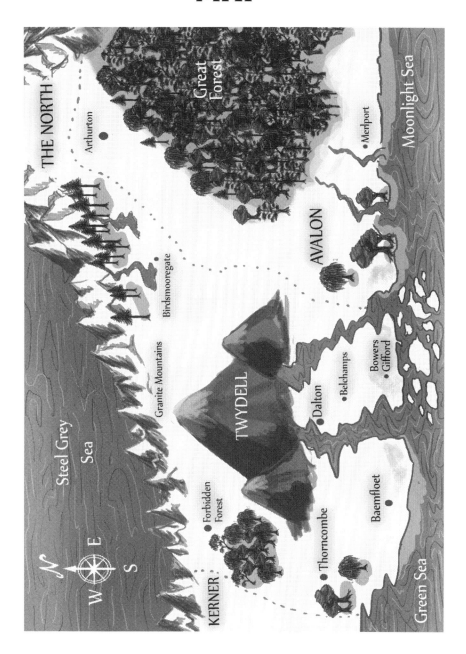

Prologue

Mankind had been foolish and destructive for far too long. It was with deep sadness that many fairies, elves, and witches made the decision to leave Briton and travel to a new home. Full of hope, they sought a land where nature flourished and all beings could live in harmony. Indeed, the witches were very much afraid that, if they did not leave Briton, their kind would be exterminated by man, who feared their magic and healing powers.

Men were content to war with one another over the slightest quarrel. They were concerned more with wealth than well-being. They had gradually destroyed many of the creatures of the forest so that only one lonely unicorn survived the wicked onslaught. Even mighty animals like the auroch and the mammoth had been hunted to extinction.

Merlin, the wizard, had sought and found a land rich in flora and fauna where he believed magical beings could live in peace. Since finding this new land, the magical beings had built a fleet of sturdy ships. They had been helped by a small group of men and women with kind hearts, who had been persecuted in Briton and who also wanted to find a new and happy home.

For many years, at each full moon, a party of the travellers had sailed to their new world. This coming night would see the last party to leave Briton.

That morning, Maud, Queen of the Fairies, and Elvira, Queen of the Witches, had searched for a four-leafed clover in the meadow. Lennox, the last of the unicorns, trotted along beside them. A four-leafed clover is always a token of good luck. However, a four-leafed clover picked in the morning dew after a unicorn has run through the meadow in which it grew, enables the creation of an even more powerful good-luck charm. The birds of the air had helped the two women find the clover leaf and now hovered above them, keeping watch, ready to raise the alarm in case of danger. The two women hurried away with Lennox. Later, in the safety of Elvira's hut, which was well hidden in the forest, they set the four-leafed clover in a clear wax. Lennox had further obliged by shedding a tear, which, once dropped into the setting wax, would provide even greater enhancement to the spells cast by the two queens. This powerful charm would be carried on the leader ship to bring good luck when it sailed from Briton that night.

While mortal men slept in their beds, three ships slid into a secluded cove on the British coast. Their waiting passengers quickly embarked, and the ships sailed away just as they had appeared: silently, like ghost ships skimming across the sea. Each craft had a hull of intricately carved mahogany and three masts on which fifteen white sailcloths waved proudly in the night breeze. The ships followed the moonlit path which sparkled on the rippling waters of the mighty ocean. They sailed as far as the eye could see from the shore, and then, at the point where the ocean disappeared into the sky, the ships lifted from the sea into the air. A light was shining from a far-away star, and the ships sailed towards its brightness. Their sails flapped in the wind, just as if the crafts were sailing on water.

The faces of the passengers looked up, towards their destination, full of hope and rapture. None felt fear because their journey had been meticulously planned and they carried with them the powerful good-luck charm. However, they still felt a certain sorrow to think that they were leaving the place where they had lived all their lives. The humans, in particular, felt sad that they were leaving friends and family behind, but they knew that if they were to stay in Briton, their lives would be in danger.

Day after day, the ships sailed through the air. Each dawn, as the starlight faded, the cool of the night was replaced by a warming sun. One morning, as the sun rose, the travellers could see a luscious green land with veins of blue water in the distance. A ripple of excitement spread throughout the ships as their passengers leaned over the deck or climbed the masts to get a better view. As they drew nearer, the outline of the land, with its meandering rivers, grew more distinct. At last, they could see a sandy beach in front of vast grasslands dotted with small copses. In the distance stood a dense forest.

Lennox pawed the deck of the ship with his hoof. He could smell the scent of other unicorns, drifting on the breeze, out from the forest. His wife and children had been slain by men seeking to sell their silvery horns and white skins for profit. Lennox had been lonely for a long time; he yearned for the companionship of others like himself.

The enchanted vessels descended gradually in the direction of the ocean below. Smiles widened on the faces of the travellers as the new land grew closer and closer. In happy accord, many of the witches took to their broomsticks and fairies to their wings. They flew alongside the ships, eager and excited to reach their new home. The witches laughed and sang, as time and again, they soared up in the air and then dipped down towards the sea. Some carried the tiny elves, who could not fly, as passengers on their brooms.

Fairy wings fluttered as they rose towards the sails; some sat or stood on the masts, while others just flew alongside. Sunlight caught the many colours in their translucent wings and reflected on the ripples of the shimmering ocean below. It was as if all the painted glass in a shattered kaleidoscope floated on the sea.

As the flying vessels landed on the water, the sails were lowered. Elves and humans jumped down from the ships and into small boats awaiting their arrival, whence they were taken ashore by oarsmen. The magical beings with wings and broomsticks flew ahead of them.

The gangplank was lowered, and Lennox stepped down into a slightly larger boat waiting especially for him. The boat creaked under the unicorn's weight. Lennox was so excited that he found it hard to stand still, making it difficult for the human oarsmen to keep the boat from overturning. However, when Lennox sensed that the sea was sufficiently shallow, he jumped down into the water and cantered towards the beach. White surf splashed over his silky body as he made his way towards dry land.

The travellers chattered and laughed as they made their way ashore. Many of those who had made the journey before them were waiting to greet the new arrivals. A cacophony of voices filled the air until, as if in unison, all attention was drawn to a tall, imposing figure on the beach. The waiting figure had stood for many hours, watching the ships as they sailed towards their destination.

"Welcome to Avalon, my friends." As Merlin's loud voice was heard, the new arrivals stood in silence and awe of the mighty wizard. The sorcerer stood tall and proud. His satin cloak, flapping in the morning breeze, glistened with all the colours of the rainbow. He held a long staff in his right hand, which he lifted high, in greeting to the newcomers. The end of the staff was encrusted with a round crystal from which emanated a purple glow that embraced all around.

Maud, Queen of the Fairies; Elvira, Queen of the Witches; and Allarond, King of the Elves, took their places beside Merlin.

A middle-aged man, who had been sitting on a rock a little way behind Merlin, forced himself to stand. His face grimaced with pain as he used both hands to push himself up. He steadied himself for a while before limping forward to take up his place alongside the other leaders.

Surprised looks appeared on the faces of the older men and women who had just arrived in Avalon. They could hardly believe their eyes to see the crippled man who stood beside the magical leaders. They pointed and smiled, and then the men bowed and the women curtseyed. Although he was more advanced in years and scarred by war, they recognised the man as Arthur, once King of the Britons. He had been a good king, and they had believed he was killed in battle. They had even mourned Arthur's death. However, Merlin had placed the near-dead king into a small boat and set it to sail for Avalon. The injured man had been nursed back to life by fairies and witches. Now, the people from Briton were overjoyed to see that their king still lived.

"This is our new home," Merlin said. "Never more shall we return to Briton. Avalon is a good and beautiful place. All the creatures which once roamed Briton are plentiful here, as are the plants we have used in our remedies and spells for millennia. Those who arrived before you have started to build new homes, and the men have started to plough the fields and plant crops. Our little settlement has become a village; one day, it will be a town. As our population grows, there will be more settlements, more villages, and more towns.

"We will endeavour to make our home a happy one, where our descendants will live in peace and harmony with each other. Nevertheless, we should remember that no matter how much goodwill we have come here with, there will always be an element of mischief and evil embedded in some hearts. Therefore, we must have a system of law, punishment, and reward. Each of our leaders – Maud, Elvira, Allarond, Arthur, and I – will be responsible for the behaviour of each of our kind. But enough now! It is time to reunite with your kinfolk and friends. You need to rest after such a long journey. Tonight, we will celebrate."

The magical beings followed those who had come to greet them, whilst the men and women let King Arthur take their lead.

Lennox trotted up to Merlin and nuzzled the old man's wizened face. Wizard and beast exchanged a few words in Unicornian. The beautiful white animal then briefly rose up on his hind legs, whinnied his goodbye, and galloped across the grassland towards the distant forest.

The people of Avalon watched the splendid creature race to find the unicorns of the unknown forest which stood in the distance. They waved their fond goodbyes. Some shouted, "Good luck", but few thought he would need it, for they all felt how fortunate they were to be in this new land – the country now known as Avalon.

Chapter 1 – Avalon

The new arrivals gazed in awe at their new surroundings. The spot that Merlin and Arthur had chosen to build their new village was on a long stretch of grassland. Colourful flowers had sprung up among the vast meadows – wild pansies, cowslips, daisies, scarlet pimpernel, to name but a few. The flowers mankind struggled to grow in the gardens in Briton grew in wild abundance in Avalon. As the bluebells and daffodils withered and fell, they were replaced by lupins, blue geraniums, and lavender, which contrasted boldly with the green meadow.

Woodbine and honeysuckle intertwined in the wild fuchsia, which formed hedgerows and provided shade for the blackberries and raspberries to flourish. Pheasants, partridges, and all sorts of birds of the air feasted on the ripened berries.

It was not hard to spot deer, hares, or rabbits as they chomped sweet meadow grass and clover. A herd of wild horses also grazed in the meadows. When the sun was too hot to bear, the herd sheltered beneath the cherry trees which grew along the river's edge.

Several woods and small copses dotted the vast meadows. These were bordered by the sea on one side, a river on another; a deep forest lay in the distance behind.

The new village was to be called Merlport, in honour of Merlin, who had found the land of Avalon. Whilst the humans were more than happy to settle in Merlport, it was not unusual for a witch or a wizard to prefer privacy. Many decided to build homes further afield or in the woodland undergrowth. Large, strong leaves and carefully placed broken branches provided comfortable homes. What's more, a home in the remote countryside meant that there were no complaints from neighbours when they brewed smelly potions in steaming cooking pots on open fires.

Fairies and elves had no need of a village or a house made of stone. They were small and fragile, and thus always a little concerned about the clumsiness of larger beings. The footstep of a human could easily squash a fairy or elf, so they preferred to dwell in the meadows and the shrubs. Some found large toadstools, which they hollowed out and made into homes for themselves. Others made little houses out of leaves and twigs, carefully hiding them from view by cunning and magic. Water fairies found shelter near ponds, where water lilies spread like stepping stones from one bank to another.

Those of the earlier arrivals who preferred village life had set to work building houses. Near the site Arthur and Merlin had chosen were heaps of stones that looked as if they had been used for houses before. However, Merlin and other wizards and witches had flown over the land for more than a hundred miles, time and time again. They had seen no sign of humans. There were plenty of bison, mammoths, horses, and other types of animals, but no human beings.

The new village of Merlport started to take form. Houses were built of the stone left by former inhabitants. Timber was taken from the nearby copses, to build the skeleton roofs to which small bundles of hay or clumps of mud were attached. Some of the new dwellings surrounded what was now the village square. This was a busy little place because a well had been constructed in the centre of the square.

Some people had planted flowers round their houses and in window boxes to make their new homes pleasing to the eye. Travellers on the ships had brought seeds. These had been sown either in small gardens, next to the houses, or in enclosures. One enclosure held a sea of sweet corn; potatoes and carrots grew in another, whilst small gardens boasted plants like asparagus and lettuce.

Roads were just dust tracks, but the children gathered shells from the beach and crushed them to make shingle. The shingle was then sprinkled on the roads to prevent them from being so muddy when it rained.

Today had been dry and sunny, so the village square was just right for this evening's celebrations to welcome the newcomers.

A young man stood beneath the cliff with his two friends, watching the new arrivals. He was a good-looking lad who stood at least six inches taller than either of his friends. His name was Edward-Arthur, and he was the illegitimate son of King Arthur.

It had never been planned for Edward to come to Avalon. He was to have remained with his mother in Briton. They had lived in the small village where his mother grew up and where she thought she had many friends. Few knew the identity of the boy's father, and it was thought that the lad was out of harm's way there. Merlin had arranged for the local wizards and witches to keep an eye on the boy and his mother in order to ensure their safety. However, one day, Edward's mother was drowned in a stream whilst the boy was playing. It was thought that the boy and his mother had been betrayed by so-called friends seeking Saxon gold.

Fearing for the boy's life, Esmerelda, the daughter of Queen Elvira, took action. She and her young warlock friend, Tannus, rescued Edward and took him to Avalon. He had been living here with his father and stepmother for six years now.

Arthur had married a witch named Gilda, who'd nursed him back to life after Merlin brought him to Avalon. They had a daughter, Rosalie, who was two years younger than Edward. Edward was very happy with his life in Avalon. When he first arrived in Avalon, his father was almost a stranger to Edward, for he had not seen Arthur in many years. Nevertheless, blood is thicker than water, and father and son built a strong bond over the ensuing years. Edward also grew close to his stepmother and half-sister. However, the young man had a burning desire to return to Briton one day. He was sure that his mother had been murdered, and he was determined to find out the truth and seek revenge.

Edward never spoke to anyone about his wish to return to Briton; it was a secret buried deep within his heart. Today, he was content to watch the newcomers.

Edward watched his father push himself up from the rock on which he sat. He could see the pain in his father's face whenever the prematurely aged Arthur stood up. The crippled man always waddled for a few paces before getting into his lame stride.

Edward had come with his friends to see the last of the flying ships arrive. Many had arrived over the years, but he always felt the same excitement when he watched them descend into the ocean. On this occasion, however, he felt a certain sadness to think these were the last people to arrive in Avalon.

He listened patiently to Merlin's speech. At last, the great wizard finished speaking. Edward had heard the speech so many times over the years that he could almost repeat it word for word.

Before leading his people away from the beach, Arthur spoke to them. He was brief because some already had friends and relatives in Avalon. Many Avalonians had come to greet their friends and kinfolk, and they were eager to catch up on lost time. "We will meet tomorrow and talk together," their king promised. "But please remember that we are all equal here. No one bends a knee to me anymore, and I do not wish anyone to do so. I wish only for a land of peace and harmony. Now I will take you to your new homes, and I look forward to seeing you at this evening's celebrations."

As the new arrivals followed his father, Edward spotted two girls about the same age as he was. "They look nice," he mumbled to his two friends, Alexander and Andrew.

"I like the taller one of the two, with the springy red hair," remarked Alexander.

"Well, that's all right then, Alex," Andrew said with a smile. "I prefer the plump little blonde. Hard luck, Edward. There's only two, so you'll have to fight Tannus for Esmerelda."

"What? Esmerelda?" Edward pretended to choke with laughter. He was often teased about his friendship with Esmerelda, who could be quite a formidable young witch. "Esmie's more like a bossy big sister to me. Tannus is welcome to her. I feel sorry for him sometimes."

Of course, that wasn't really how Edward felt about Esmerelda. It was true: the young witch was like an older sister to him, and she was bossy, to say the least. Her presence made most humans nervous. However, Edward had travelled to Avalon with her, and he knew that there was a softer side to her character that most people did not see. He loved her almost as much as he loved his younger half-sister, Rosalie.

"There'll be a good party tonight," Andrew commented. "I wonder whether the new girls can dance."

"All girls can dance," replied Alex. "It just depends whether they are too tired. I hear men complaining a lot that women are too tired to have any fun."

"Well, I'll be dancing with Connie, the baker's daughter." Edward smiled confidently. "I won't fight you for the two newcomers."

Edward noticed the two newly arrived girls nudging each other and pointing towards him. Rather than upset his friends, he pretended not to notice the girls' interest in him. Instead, he headed towards Connie, who was standing on the beach and welcoming the new arrivals.

"Are you coming to the celebrations tonight, Con?" he asked.

"Wouldn't miss it for a new world," replied Connie. As she smiled, her nose crinkled, and Edward admired the golden freckles on her nose and the twinkle in her hazel eyes. She reminded him of his mother. "I love to see the spellfolk dancing – especially the wizzwits. The wizzwits look so funny."

"Be careful they don't hear you calling them spellfolk or wizzwits." Edward smiled back at her. "They might be offended and turn you into a frog."

"Oh, I'm sure they know what we call them," Connie replied. "In fact, I've heard them refer to us as the plainfolk."

"Really?" Edward raised his eyebrows, feigning surprise. "I must ask Esmerelda whether she refers to me as a plainfolk. Perhaps she calls me a plainman."

"Plainboy, more like!" Connie retorted. "Although, perhaps you're not so plain." The girl's cheeks turned pink as she paid Edward the compliment.

"Plain or not, I can do a fine jig when the music starts. Will you dance with me tonight, Con?"

Connie blushed an even deeper shade of red but nodded her head enthusiastically before hurrying off.

That night, a feast was prepared in the village square, in honour of the newcomers. A vegetable stew laced with herbs boiled in a huge cauldron. Fresh bread, puddings, and pies had been baked. Away from the vegetable stew, because many of the Avalonians did not eat meat, a wild boar roasted on a spit. The delicious aroma of fresh food cooking filled the air.

Witches and wizards joined the party. A few fairies and elves sat on the rooftops to watch the celebrations, but most disappeared into the surrounding meadows and woodland.

Hops grew in abundance in Avalon, and there were plenty of honeybees, so a sweet mead had been prepared. However, the men generally preferred their beer neat and undiluted by honey. For those who did not wish to wake up with an aching head, there was plenty of fresh spring water and apple juice.

Pipers piped, fiddlers fiddled, and a rather fat man squeezed an accordion. The fat man had a loud but melodious voice, and it didn't take long for other less-harmonious voices to join in.

Soon few were able to stop their feet from tapping in time to the music. One of the men grasped his wife's arm and led her into a space where they started to dance. It only takes one couple to get up and dance for others to follow. The couples danced around the stone well which stood in the middle of the square. Some used steps they had been taught, and others just jigged about in ways that they thought looked good.

It didn't take long for the wizzwits to join the humans – or *plainfolk*, as they called them – in the square. The wizzwits wore their long cloaks and pointed hats. Their dancing seemed to consist of bobbing up and down as they skipped round in a circle, in time to the music. In the firelight, their tall hats cast long shadows across the square. The eerie shadows danced up and down against the surrounding buildings. Smoke from the fires drifted upwards, towards the sky, taking with it bright sparks from the smouldering logs.

Edward grabbed Connie by the hand and led her into a space in the square. They linked arms as they joined other merrymakers in a reel. The couple turned and twirled until they were dizzy. They recovered from their bouts of dizziness by gulping down mugs of sweet mead before re-joining the dancers.

Alex and Andrew had already led the two girls they'd seen earlier into the dancing. However, Andrew was quite a clumsy fellow and kept treading on the plump little blonde girl's toes. She eventually got fed up with him and went off to find her parents, leaving the poor boy standing alone and looking miserable.

Apart from Andrew, everyone else seemed happy. Laughter and singing filled the air.

Edward and Connie danced till the early hours of the morning. Connie had turned to the fresh water for sustenance, but Edward continued to enjoy the sweet taste of mead whenever they took a break. As the evening progressed, Edward's head swirled with a strange sensation he had never experienced before.

Edward couldn't remember finding his way home, but he must have done so because he could hear his stepmother calling him from downstairs.

"Get up, Edward!" shouted Gilda. "You are supposed to be helping to cut trees in the Great Forest today."

"Alright. I'm up," he called back although he was, in fact, still in bed.

Edward made an effort to get up, only to lie straight back down again because the room was spinning. His tousled mop of dark hair spread back over the pillow. His head throbbed. Last night, the sweet mead had tasted good, and the more he drank, the more he seemed to enjoy himself. He tried to open his eyes, but they stung, and so he closed them again. At the time, it seemed like a good idea to keep them closed for a bit longer. If he lay in bed for a just a few minutes more, he thought he might awake refreshed.

Edward wanted to get up. For many years, he had looked forward to visiting the Great Forest. When he was younger, he and his friends had attempted to visit the forest several times, yearning to explore its hidden depths. They wanted to climb trees and build a secret den. If they had a den, they would have a place to call their own. They could laugh and tell jokes, without any adults telling them what they should be doing. However, on each occasion, the boys had been seen by the wizards, who had ordered them to head back to the village.

"You boys must learn to wait," the wizards had said firmly. "We need to investigate that forest properly. There's something not quite right about it."

"When are you going to investigate it?" the boys would ask, almost pleading.

"When there are enough of us here to form an investigative party!" the wizards had always retorted as they shooed the boys home.

Edward was just like any other boy: when told not to do something, it always made the yearning to actually do it even worse. Now, the day he had longed for since his first attempted visit had actually arrived. He had planned to get up early. Perhaps it was the headache, or the thought of exploring the mysteries of the forest, which made Edward fall into a slumber. Whatever it was, he dreamed of a forest with a unicorn and other strange beings.

Edward was snapped out of his reverie by cold water dripping on his face. He woke up with a start, opening his eyes to see Gilda standing above him. His stepmother was attempting to rouse him by wringing out a wet cloth over his face.

"Wake up, sleepyhead! It was half an hour ago I called you. You said you were getting up, but, instead, I find you're back in bed! Your father and the other men are almost ready to leave. You'll hold everyone up if you don't hurry!"

Edward pulled on his clothes and made his way downstairs.

"There's scrambled egg and mushrooms in the pan," his stepmother said.

Normally, Edward would have devoured his favourite breakfast with relish, but this morning the smell made him feel sick. He gulped down a mug of water and hurried outside, where his father and a group of other people were gathering.

"Good morning, young man," Merlin greeted him with a wry smile. "Good night, was it?"

"Very good," replied Edward.

He was busy tucking in his shirt when he saw Connie across the road. She waved to him and gave him a wide smile.

Edward crossed the road to speak to her.

The men in the working party busied about, checking that they had all the equipment they needed and that axes had been adequately sharpened. Satisfied that all was as it should be, they began to make their way up the hill towards the Great Forest.

"Come on, Edward," his father's voice boomed.

The tone of his father's voice made the words' meaning clear to Edward. Mumbling his goodbye to Connie, he ran after the working party making its way to the Great Forest.

The New Land

Chapter 2 – The Giants of the Great Forest

At first, the Avalonians only took the timber they needed from the nearby woods. The trees they cut were carefully selected by Willy the Wood Wizard. Both the humans and the wizzwits were keen not to destroy the trees of Avalon without good reason. They knew that trees were needed to help create the rain which filled the rivers and watered the crops. They were also aware that they would need to share the trees with wildlife as well as future generations of their own kind.

As the building of the village grew nearer to what they now called the Great Forest, they decided it was time to start taking its trees.

Today was the day that a party of men and wizards, including Willy the Wood Wizard, Merlin, and Arthur, went to explore the forest and take its first trees.

Edward, Alex, and Andrew had been brought along to help, as they had done previously when trees were felled in the small copses around Merlport. Tree felling was hard work, and all the boys were expected to assist. To be fair, the trio had never shied away from work, and today they were every bit as eager as before to visit the Great Forest.

Edward always considered Willy to be a strange little fellow. He spent a lot of time muttering to himself. Often, when the boys tried to speak to him, he appeared not to hear. None of the humans seemed to understand how he selected the trees to be cut, but Edward had noticed that before they were allowed to put an axe to a tree, the wood wizard appeared to say a little prayer.

As they trekked up the hill, the boys heard an old, white-haired wizard, Wormald the Wise, chastising Merlin. "We should have sent in an exploratory party before going to the forest. We don't know what dangers may belie us."

Andrew rolled his eyes, and Edward grinned at him.

"We have flown over the forest several times, and not a person to be seen," Merlin replied to Wormald's concerns. "We are only going to the edge of the wood; we are not entering its depths."

"Nevertheless, we should have a standard procedure before entering new territory and putting our working party at risk. These plainfolk have no magic with which to protect themselves."

Alex silently imitated Wormald's concerns.

Although Edward was amused by his friend's mimicry, he shook his head. His father had always made it clear that the wizzwits should be treated with respect; after all, Gilda, Edward's own stepmother, was a witch.

Andrew giggled at Alex's impression of Wormald.

Although Edward was trying to keep a straight face, he was finding it very hard to do so. If Edward laughed at Wormald and his father saw, he would not be amused. The clear air had eased Edward's aching head, and now he ran ahead, needing to avoid his father's gaze.

The mysterious forest had always been like a magnet to the three boys, so Alex and Andrew did not hesitate in following their friend.

The rest of the party shouted for the boys to return.

Better to be told off for running ahead than to be scolded by my father for laughing at a wizard, Edward told himself.

The youths started climbing trees and swinging on branches, like big children at play. Suddenly, Edward felt uneasy, as if he were being watched. The laughter in his face dissolved, replaced by a look of apprehension. Casting his eyes round the dense undergrowth, he saw nothing untoward. In spite of the fact that everything seemed as he might have expected, he slid down from the branch on which he was perched. His two companions must have shared his unspoken concerns because, after exchanging glances, the three friends re-joined the others.

The party had just reached the edge of the wood and had already selected a tree which seemed suitable for roofing timbers.

Willy was just talking to the tree to see if it was ready to be cut when a loud, bellowing voice asked the party, "What do you think you are doing?!"

The voice was accompanied by a huge giant who appeared from behind a cluster of trees.

As Merlin and the others looked into the depths of the forest, their eyes grew accustomed to the darkness within, and other large shadowy figures also became apparent. The figures moved forward to reveal large men clad in the same manner of dress as humans. The leader was a red-headed man who wore a green woollen vest tucked into brown dungarees. He had a round face with rosy cheeks. Bushy eyebrows knitted together above enquiring eyes. He stood with his feet placed firmly on the ground, one hand on his hip, and the other holding what looked like a large club over his shoulder.

Edward heard his father speak. His voice was perfectly calm. "Good day to you, sir. My name is Arthur. Our people started to travel to this beautiful land some years ago now. My friend, the wizard Merlin, searched the land to see if anyone else lived here, for we had no wish to steal."

"I saw no one on my visits, and neither did any of my companions," said Merlin. "I am somewhat confused because if my old eyes deceive me, my other senses generally don't. I had no sense of any other race of people – although they have clearly lived here in the past."

Merlin lifted his hands in a gesture of explanation. However, Edward noticed that Wormald and the other wizards, except Willy, were surreptitiously moving their own hands towards their sleeves, where they kept their wands.

"Why did we not sense these giants before?" Merlin whispered to Willy, who stood a little way behind him.

Willy stepped forward, making no attempt to retrieve his wand. He spoke loudly so all could hear. "Ah, you did not sense the mighty Zog and his clan of giants because they are at one with the forest. They have lived in the forest for so long that they belong to it, and so their presence was hidden." Willy bowed his head slowly as a sign of respect to the leader of the giants.

"So, if you didn't know we lived here, how d'you know me name, you weird little man?"

"I am a wood wizard." Willy smiled, and as he did so, his wizened face, which much resembled the gnarled bark of a tree, crinkled. His hair was a greenish grey, and he wore a brown pointed hat and cloak. When he stood next to a tree, he became almost invisible.

Willy continued. "I talk to the trees. They tell me when they are sick and need help. They tell me when they are ready to be cut down to make room for others. This old oak tree here, which has spread its branches wide, has told me that he has shed many acorns, but for more than a century, none have grown because his saplings cannot see the light from the sun. His roots are failing now, and the time has come for him to make room for new growth.

"Sometimes, when I talk to trees, they tell me that their bodies are to be used for a special purpose. This old oak has told me that he wishes his body to be used to make a likeness of the brave warrior whose name is Zog, who stopped the cutting of many trees before their time. Forgive me, Lord Zog, but I believe you already know that your days on this land are limited. This tree wishes to mark its respect for you by using its body to create an image in your likeness."

"Yes, I am Zog." The giant frowned. He seemed unsure whether to believe the wood wizard; nor did he admit that he too knew that his life would not be for much longer.

"That beech tree over there is telling me that his time has come to retire too. He would like his trunk to be used to create the image of another brave warrior, Greatog, who died in battle, but I do not understand some of the words he uses."

Zog looked suspicious but nodded. "My father was Greatog. He died from the injuries he suffered whilst fighting the Trajaens who raided this coast. It was the Trajaens who slaughtered the small people, like you, who used to live here."

"Ah, I know how it is to suffer from the injuries of war," Arthur said now. Looking into the giant's face, he recognised the pain of a kindred spirit enduring the agonies left by battle. "We knew that someone had lived here before because we found the stone which must have once been their houses. Please tell us what happened to the people who once occupied this land, for we have seen no one else except for your good selves."

Arthur was concerned. He had fought enough battles in Briton. He was not sure that he had the strength to wield a sword again. Nevertheless, he knew that few could match his planning and strategy in the battlefield. Even fewer could match his negotiation skills at the end of the fight. Arthur was still a valuable asset to the Avalonians. He was anxious to live peacefully beside the giants. He wanted to find out more about the people who once lived in the place where Merlport was now situated, and also about the people known as Trajaens, who had raided the coast.

Arthur told Edward to listen carefully to what the giants told them and to learn from what he heard.

Edward nodded dutifully.

Avalonians and giants sat down in a circle in the grass meadow. The men had brought jugged hare, elfin bread, and spring water for their lunch. The giants had brought bread, cheese, venison, and red apples. They had also brought some cider, which they shared, somewhat sparingly, with the Avalonians.

Edward sat with Alex and Andrew, and the three lads listened intently. They were still wary of the giants, but the huge men seemed agreeable enough, at least for the time being. All the boys were keen to learn about the possible enemy which the giants were telling them about. The old king had given Edward and his two friends brief lessons on how to use a sword. They had always wanted more lessons, but the priority in Merlport had always been to grow food and build houses. How would they defend themselves if the Trajaens attacked again?

The giants told the party from the village, "People similar to you newcomers lived here before. We've also seen those tiny people with wings, who resembled butterflies, but we've not seen 'em for many years now." The giants went on to say they thought this was a pity because they liked to watch the tiny people flying in and out of the forest. They also said the pretty little things never did any harm. However, although they had heard of them, they had never seen any of the strange people with tall hats, who rode on brooms, in these parts before.

"I wouldn't mind one of them contraptions. It'd save a lot of walking," Zog said, looking directly at Willy's broom.

Merlin explained that it was not the broom that could fly but the special skill of the person riding it. Regrettably, those skills could not be taught to those born without magic.

Zog looked disappointed but continued with his tale.

The giants had lived peacefully next to the people who used to dwell in the stone houses and had called themselves

Brewins. The bears of the forest, which also walked on two legs, had been named bruins after them.

"They didn't bother us, and we didn't bother them!" one of the giants stated firmly. "They never came into our forest, and we rarely leave it. We don't like getting wet, so we stay as far away from the sea as possible."

The giants went on to tell them that people lived in the land known as Twydell, to the west of this place now called Avalon. Twydell was ruled by King Frederrick and Queen Elise, who seemed friendly enough. It was a land made up of three tall mountains and two large valleys running in between. The valleys turned into meadow as they spread down towards the sea. However, much of the land along the south coast was marshy and was occupied by a small race of human beings known as the Marsh People.

A few giants lived on the far side of Twydell, near a small country called Kerner. Kerner was ruled by King Jeffrey and Queen Shirley-Poppy. The Kernans were not as friendly as the Twydellers, according to Zog, but his people hadn't been in contact with the Kernans for many a year. "Not in my lifetime, anyways," as Zog phrased it.

Twydell had two coastlines but its northern coastline consisted of a chain of Granite Mountains which had never been crossed. Kerner was shaped like a triangle and had two vulnerable coast lines. Both Twydell and Kerner were plagued by raids from the Trajaens. Trajaens came in longboats from another land across the sea. They wore silvery covered helmets with what looked like cow horns poking out on either side. Heavy golden and silver bands adorned their muscular arms and necks. They had brown skin and hair the colour of ebony, as were their long moustaches and beards.

"Which they never comb!" said one of the giants, proudly stroking his own silky ginger chin growth.

19

The Trajaens were strong "for their kind", the giants explained, and they carried many weapons. Not just swords, but axes, bows and arrows, and long spears.

"Them fools, Frederrick and Jeffrey, they only paid 'em to go away!" Zog spoke with anger.

The other giants nodded.

Zog continued. "The Trajaens just used the money to go and buy more weapons to attack Twydell and Kerner all over again. They stole their corn, they stole their jewellery, and they even stole their young people and made 'em into slaves!

"But it wasn't just the Twydeller or Kernan fools they attacked. Oh no! They came back 'ere and attacked the Brewins. The Brewins didn't have no fine armies like Twydell or Kerner. They stood no chance against those Trajaens with their shiny new weapons. It was like lambs going to the slaughter.

"We didn't interfere at first. Thought it was none of our business, like. What arguments go on between the small peoples, nothin' to do with us. We don't get involved.

"We let the Trajaens live in the village for a while, with their Brewin prisoners. But then they started to cut down trees from our forest to make more boats, well, that was a different matter. Those are our trees! We weren't 'aving none of that! They didn't have no tree talkers like you lot. It was just cut, cut, cut!"

Zog described how the giants came out of the forest to confront the Trajaens. The Trajaens tried to drive the giants back into the forest by unleashing arrows at them. He clenched his fist as he spoke. "They went and tied rags to their arrows and set fire to them. The fools set the undergrowth alight. We thought our forest was gonna go up in flames! We could have lost everything – our families, our homes, our livestock, as well as the trees. As luck would have it, the heavens opened up, and the rain fell in torrents."

The giants went on to tell the Avalonians that instead of being driven back into the forest, they were fuelled by anger. They didn't often leave the forest, but, on this occasion, they advanced towards the Trajaens. Many giants were killed or injured in the onslaught, including Greatog, but they chased the Trajaens back into the sea.

Zog continued the story. "It was all too late for the Brewins. Those who hadn't already been slaughtered by the Trajaens, were taken as slaves. When we came out of the forest, the few Brewins left were forced on board the longboats and taken away. There was only one boat left by the time we got to the shore because when they realised what they were up against, they ran for their lives, so they did! We don't like the sea. We don't like getting wet, but we went in after 'em and got hold of the last boat. We lifted it up and tipped it into the water."

The giants laughed at the memory.

"Them there Trajaens, they just sank into the sea and got swept away. There was no way they could swim with all them golden bands round their arms and necks.

"Next, we smashed up the houses to make sure that nobody lived in 'em again. Nobody until you came along, that is. We thought we'd watch and wait."

"I see," said Merlin thoughtfully. "But, why did you do nothing to stop us from rebuilding?"

Zog smiled. "Well, if the Trajaens come back, you'll be here to see 'em off, won't you?"

"They'll be back," one giant added, nodding his head sagely. "They took a beating, but they'll be back!"

The others giants agreed.

"No doubt about it." Zog was serious now. "That's why we don't mind you settling here. If you can keep the Trajaens off this land, you can stay here. That is, you can stay here, as long as you don't cut trees from our forest without our say-so. You will also not hunt the animals in our forest because we are big people, with big appetites, and there is only so much food to go round."

Merlin felt a sudden pang of fear. "Do you hunt unicorns too?"

"No," replied Zog scornfully. "What fool would hunt unicorns? Don't you know that it's bad luck to kill a magical beast like that?"

"Indeed." Merlin breathed a sigh of relief. "We brought a friend here with us. A unicorn named Lennox. Lennox is a splendid creature. He was the last of his kind in Briton, the place where we used to live. He hoped that he would find more of his kind here."

The giants laughed.

A ginger-bearded giant with a loud rumbling guffaw told him that a new white unicorn stallion had arrived in the forest. Tyzon, the leader of the forest herd, had not been happy about the appearance of a rival. Tyzon and the newcomer were exact opposites. Tyzon was a sturdy black unicorn, much bulkier than the new white arrival. Nevertheless, the new stallion was a powerful force to be reckoned with, and both were capable of seriously injuring the other. There had been a clash of horns and then a stand-off. Neither was injured, but some of the mares had left the herd and galloped off with the newcomer.

"Not a bad thing to happen!" Zog laughed. "The unicorns could do with some new blood, and Tyzon is a bit full of himself. He needed to be brought down a peg or two."

"Please tell us about the other creatures which live here," said Merlin. "Are there any dragons or phoenix?"

The giants told him that there were dragons in the Twydell mountains, which sometimes stole sheep and goats, but were rarely seen in this area. The Trajaens had stolen nearly all of the Brewins' stock. What was left of the Brewins' herds had wandered off into the wild.

The giants were not sure what a phoenix was. However, when the wizards told them it was a large colourful bird, they nodded. They described how a bird with blue, green, and red feathers had risen out of the ashes of the Brewins' settlement.

The wizards exchanged knowing looks. A phoenix rising from the ashes foretold that the Brewins' town would be rebuilt.

"It flew off in that direction." One of the giants pointed towards the west. "My cousin said he had seen it on the plains on the other side of Twydell."

"We do see the thunderbirds sometimes," said one of the giants. "That's one of the reasons our ancestors liked to live in the forest. Thunderbirds are big enough to carry off one of your children. They're even strong enough to carry off one of ours!"

"Amazing." Merlin was interested. "I've never heard of a thunderbird before. What do they look like?"

The giants described a large bluish-grey bird of prey, which some people called the rain bird. They said that when the thunderbird flapped its wings overhead, it often sounded like thunder, and its appearance always seemed to bring heavy rain.

"When yer see the thunderbird, yer head for home and make sure all yer family's inside," the ginger-bearded giant advised. "Yer hear the flapping wings like thunder, and then yer feel the rain."

"And make sure yer cattle and sheep are in the barns, to keep 'em dry," Zog added knowingly.

Merlin asked how far it was to Twydell.

The giants told him that they could walk there in two days, so it would probably take his shorter legs four or five.

The giants made it known that they wanted to end the parley and make their way home, but Arthur still had some questions.

"Did none of the Brewins survive?"

Zog said, "Far as I know, only one girl is left here. Each time they attacked, the Trajaens took a lot of them off, across the sea, to sell as slaves – if ye can call that survival, they survived. The girl who was left was kept here as a child slave by one of the Trajaens who tried to make a home here.

"When the Trajaens knew we had the better of 'em, they either killed the slaves who were left before they ran, or put 'em on long boats to take with 'em. S'pose they thought we might make use of 'em, but we don't believe in slavery. It's a wicked trade. Anyways, the little maid managed to hide in the woods over there." Zog pointed to a small copse near the village. "She lives in a cave in the hills now. Pretty little thing but very strange. We think the animals must have taken pity on her and brought her up. She talks to wild beasts, like Willy here talks to trees!"

"She's got a pet wolf. A huge grey thing. It'll attack yer if yer go near her," Ginger-beard put in.

"She caught a wild pony and tamed it herself," added another giant.

"And she's got a pet goat," added another.

"The birds come down and feed out of the palm of her hands." An elderly giant smiled at the recollection of the young girl with birds perched on her arms and hands.

"Doesn't the wolf attack the goat or the pony?" asked Merlin.

Zog said, "No. She seems to have trained it not to hurt her pets – but it won't think twice about biting the throat of anyone or anything which tries to harm her!

"She can use a bow and arrow too. We call her Amazon, we don't know what her real name is. She refuses to talk to us. Her aim is deadly accurate. If you get too close, she'll let off an arrow, which will land at yer feet as a warning, but she could just as easily hit you in the eye with it!"

Arthur asked the giants if they would show them where the girl lived.

The giants seemed to find Arthur's request amusing.

"We'll tell ye, but we won't show yer." One of the giants chuckled. "We don't want to start a fight with the grey wolf or get hit in the eye by an arrow." He then went on to describe where the girl lived.

"Now. One final piece of business." Zog spoke seriously. "You, Willy the Wood Wizard, you reckon the trees talk to you, and that there beech tree has asked you to create an image in the likeness of my father, Greatog. Now, you've never seen Greatog. I give you my permission to cut down that beech tree, whose foliage I admit looks past its best, and so it probably does need to make way for younger saplings. But, before we allow you to enter our forest and cut down any more, I want to see this image of my father. If you are telling us the truth, and not spinning a yarn, then you'll have our permission to cut other trees, but only those that we permit you to cut."

"That sounds very reasonable to me." Merlin nodded. "Willy, how long will you need to make the image of Greatog?"

"As long as it takes," replied Willy blandly. "I have no knowledge of time when I'm carving. I simply keep going until I know it will reach the old tree's satisfaction."

"Then how will our giant friends know when it's finished?" asked Arthur. "We don't have their permission to enter the forest to look for them."

"That's easy." Willy smiled. "I'll leave a note in the hollow of that oak tree over there. See the hole at the bottom of its trunk? I'll leave it in there."

"What do you mean a note? A note like in moosic?" Zog looked puzzled.

"No. I mean a note, as in a piece of parchment with words written on it."

"Oh, I knows what you mean. We saw them funny squiggles that the Brewins used to draw, and those Trajaens they do the same. We don't bother with all that. Just leave a sock in the tree. Leave a pink one, to make sure we spot it and it just don't get hidden inside."

"But, what if a fairy or elf or animal carries it off?" asked one of the wizards.

"Well, put some stones inside. No small creature will be able to move it then."

"Right," said Willy. "I will put a pink sock, filled with stones, in the hollow base of that oak tree as soon as the image is ready."

The giants watched and helped as the men felled the selected beech tree. When the deed was done, they said their goodbyes and left the men to roll the great tree trunk back to Merlport.

As they rolled the tree trunk down the hill, the Avalonians pondered over the day's events.

Edward was mesmerised. As a child he had been brought to this land by witches, wizards, fairies, and elves. Today, he met giants. Would the charmed life he seemed to be leading come to an abrupt end by a Trajaen axe?

"Father, we need more sword training," Edward said. As the words left his mouth, he realised that they sounded more like a command than a request.

"Yes," agreed Arthur. "Now that we have no trees to cut for a while, we will start training again. Tonight, when you get back, you can speak to all the able-bodied men and ask them to bring what weapons they have to the village square first thing tomorrow morning."

"Mmm, good idea," Wormald the Wise said authoritatively. "I think I will call our brethren together and start practising defensive spells."

For once, the boys did not make fun of the old wizard behind his back.

Chapter 3 – Merlin Plans a Trip

The men of Merlport practised with wooden swords while Arthur watched, barking instructions from his seat.

It was clear that Edward and the other youths relished the activity. They made it known, at every opportunity, that they thought it would be better to practise with real swords. However, even if they had all been sufficiently skilled to practise with blades which cut, rather than sticks that bruised, there would not have been enough swords for everyone. To this end, Arthur commissioned the blacksmith to make enough swords, axes, and maces to arm all the men in Merlport.

Meanwhile, Wormald the Wise sat with a group of wizards, huddled in a nearby copse, away from the sound of clattering wood. An invisible circle surrounded them, which no man would be able to penetrate.

Merlin attended the meeting for a while before excusing himself. He had expected to find Willy at the meeting. However, the wood wizard had given his apologies, advising that he wanted to start creating the image of Greatog without delay.

After leaving the circle, Merlin hurried off to see Willy, but first stopped to speak to Arthur.

The king knew that the sorcerer was present, and listened to him, but kept his eyes on the duelling men as they trained.

"Well, it looks as if Willy will be busy for a few days. I think I will take a trip to Twydell. I would like to meet King Frederrick and Queen Elise. I would certainly like to know more about the dragons and thunderbirds which live there."

"Aren't you going to practise spells with Wormald?" asked Arthur.

"Do you think I need to practise spells? I'm disappointed in you, Arthur." Merlin pretended to sound surprised and hurt.

Arthur smiled.

"No. Wormald is more than capable of teaching our young warlocks a trick or two. My time would be better spent acting as an envoy to our neighbours."

Strengthening his case for the visit, the sorcerer continued. "Our neighbours may be able to give us more insight into these Trajaens. Our people have been here for some thirteen years now, but we have not been bothered by them. That would be because the first arrivals were almost all fairies and elves who might not have been noticeable to the Trajaens as they sailed along the coast. However, even from a distance, our continued building must already be visible. Of course, the Trajaens may be afraid of coming back here because they fear another defeat by the giants."

"I have never seen any boats, other than ours, out at sea," replied Arthur. "We are in a bit of an inlet here, and I suppose not too noticeable because of the surrounding hills and trees. Nonetheless, you are right. We need to find out more and build new allies."

Tongue in cheek, as he kept his eyes on the duellers, the king added, "Of course, you are obviously the best choice to act as envoy. That way, I can keep the able-bodied men here."

Merlin laughed. He liked it when his friend joked. The smile on Arthur's face made him look younger and brought back memories of the handsome knight he once was.

With a sigh, Arthur took his eyes off the men battling each other with wooden swords. He looked his most faithful advisor in the eye. "I sincerely hope that we will not have to go to war again, my friend."

"I sincerely hope not!" Merlin responded. "I will only be gone a few days. The giants said that it would take them two days to walk to the capital town of Twydell and that it would take our shorter legs four or five. It should take me less by broom."

"Then we will see you again in about a week's time." Arthur nodded and turned his head back to watch his men.

"While you are off to Twydell, and Willy is busy making his carving of Greatog, I will send a party to search for that girl. After all, it sounds as if she is a human being just like my people. Despite what the giants say about her ability to look after herself, she must be very frightened and lonely living on that mountain all alone."

"Good idea," Merlin said, nodding. "Poor young lass out there all on her own. I'll look forward to talking to her when I get back. We would all gain by knowing more about the Brewins."

Merlin said goodbye to Arthur and waved to the men practising their sword skills.

Only Andrew saw him, and he raised his sword arm to acknowledge the wizard's departure.

Edward, who was duelling with Andrew, mistook his friend's gesture as a preparation for a vertical head chop. The prince immediately thrust his wooden weapon at his friend's unguarded ribs, expecting him to step back.

Instead, Andrew fell to the ground, crying out in pain.

Arthur barked an angry rebuke at the youth. "Never take your eyes off your opponent, you fool! If that were a real sword, you would be dead by now!"

Andrew was not only bruised, but his pride was wounded too. His face turned a bright scarlet shade of embarrassment.

Edward discarded his wooden sword and fell to his knees to comfort his friend.

Merlin lowered his head in guilt, and then scurried off in the opposite direction to find Willy. He was anxious to see the wood wizard before he became too engrossed in his task. He had seen Willy at work before, and knew how difficult it would be to communicate with him once he started his project.

He found the little man arranging his tools on a bench. The felled beech tree lay in front of him.

Just in time, Merlin thought.

Merlin put his arm round Willy's shoulders and spoke to him in his most endearing terms. "My dear friend, you will be very busy for a few days. While you are engrossed in your work, may I borrow your broom, please?"

"Why can't you use your own broom?"

"I've gotten rid of mine."

"Why?"

"Oh, it was falling apart." Merlin waved his free arm, as if to provide some sort of explanation, but kept his other around Willy's shoulder. "I don't like flying now. I get stiff in the cold wind, and my eyes keep watering. I no longer enjoy it."

"So, if you don't like flying any more, why do you want to fly now?" Willy's question seemed quite reasonable.

"I need to go to Twydell," explained Merlin. He then put forward the best case for borrowing Willy's broom that he could think of. "I will act as an envoy from Avalon to Twydell. It is imperative that we find out more about our neighbours and make them our allies. There may even be more wizards who live there. Wouldn't you like to make more friends, Willy?"

"You could take one of the horses the men have captured and trained, and ride to Twydell," retorted the wood wizard, who remained unconvinced by Merlin's argument.

"Flying is much quicker and safer. I can soon fly out of the reach of hostile men, but I could not easily outride them. Besides, do you think my old bones would stand up to several days' ride on horseback? Come, Willy, my friend, lend me your broom. You won't need it before I return, and I promise I will bring it back safely."

"It's a pity we don't have any wood; we could then make you a boat, and you could cruise round the coast to Twydell."

"It's a pity we don't have wood to make me a carriage, or velvet for cushions, for then I could drive myself to Twydell in a little bit of comfort!" retorted Merlin.

"Alright," Willy agreed. "But if you damage my broom, you repair it!"

"Thank you. I knew you were a good-natured chap." Merlin smiled as he withdrew his arm from round Willy's shoulders.

Chapter 4 – Daisy; The Last of the Brewins

"This will be your first command," the king told his son. "I will listen carefully to how the men who go with you speak about your leadership when you return."

Arthur had been unsure whether to put his son in charge of the party going to look for the Brewin girl. However, after giving the matter some consideration, the king decided that it would not be a difficult task to find the girl and bring her back to civilisation. No one had travelled far from Merlport since arriving in Avalon. Most of the humans had been in the last ships to arrive. They now needed more scouting parties to investigate the outlying areas.

Edward's pride showed in his face. It wasn't because his father had chosen him to lead the group. It wasn't even the fact that he was riding the fine bay stallion his father had selected for him, when still a foal, from the wild horses which roamed the grasslands. It was the steel sword, hanging at his hip, which made him feel that he had truly become a man at last.

The prince had grown into a good-looking lad. He was tall and broad, as his father had once been. He was also thoughtful and beginning to show wisdom beyond his youth. He worked hard no matter what task he was given. His courteous manner made him well liked and respected by all.

Nevertheless, Arthur had chosen the five other men carefully. They were all experienced soldiers. They may have been past their prime, but three knew how to fire an arrow, one was a huntsman skilled in tracking, and the fifth had once been a swordsman. If Edward did not act wisely then they would advise him accordingly, without seeming to argue.

It only took a few hours to reach the hills where the giants had said the girl lived. Edward was enjoying himself. It was the first chance he'd had to ride more than a few miles on Challenger, his bay stallion. He would have loved to have urged Challenger into a gallop, but that would not have been right. The other men's mounts were more like the horses seen working in the fields; a far cry from Challenger and the fast, sleek, horses ridden by soldiers.

There were several winding paths round the hills. At each path they found, Edward looked hopefully at the tracker, who inspected the path carefully to see what kind of animal was using it.

The man would jump down off his palfrey, examine the tracks, but then look at the prince and shake his head. "Goats and sheep," he stated several times.

On one occasion, he spent more time looking at the tracks. Edward started to feel excited, but when the tracker turned and saw him looking at him anxiously he said, "Sorry, m' lord, it's the track of a large stag with a herd of a dozen does. A fine place for hunting, though."

At last, Edward heard the news he wanted. After carefully examining the prints in a fairly well-hidden path, the tracker announced, "It's a pony. The tracks are deep, as if it's carrying a rider."

"It must be the girl," declared Edward. "There are no other humans in this area, and the giants said she had a pony."

The men nodded their agreement.

The path was very narrow, and twisted round the hill. The men did not need Edward to tell them that they should leave their tired horses behind. However, they waited for their leader to give the orders. The prince jumped down from

Challenger, looked carefully at the prints the tracker showed him, and gave the order to dismount.

Edward looked at the horses and told one of the archers to stay behind and look after them whilst the others continued on foot. As Edward looked back at the track, he didn't notice the smiling and approving nods of his men. He asked the tracker to take the lead.

The path wound its way up a steep incline. Their ascent was slow because it was hard work walking uphill, and the pathway kept crumbling beneath their feet.

"Ah," said the tracker after a short distance. "Look, m' lord, here is where she dismounted.

Edward examined the track he was shown, and could indeed see the change in the depth of the hoof prints when they were pointed out to him.

At this point, Edward took the lead. He might have been a little bit vain, but he felt that the girl might not be so frightened if she set her eyes on him first. She would see him as the knight coming to her rescue, whereas the scarred and battle-hardened men who followed him might frighten her.

Just as he was rounding a bend, near the top of the hill, an arrow thudded into the ground in front of him. He gasped because the arrow was only an inch or so away from his toe. It had come from farther up the path in front of them.

He looked up but saw no one, and so he called out, "I am Edward-Arthur, son of King Arthur. The giants have told us about the terrible slaughter of the Brewins. We have come to tell you that we have built a new village on the site where you once lived. We wish you no harm, and invite you to join us. You need not hide away in a cave any more. You can return to a proper home in our village of Merlport."

Edward truly expected the girl to come out from where she was hiding and rush down the hill towards them, arms open in gratitude. He was very wrong. To his surprise, another arrow thudded into the ground in front of his feet, and he took a step back.

"We wish you no harm. We come as friends," he shouted as loud as he could, in case she had not heard him the first time.

"Go away!" the girl shouted. "Come another step nearer, and I'll kill you, no matter whose son you are!" With that, another arrow thudded into the ground alongside the others.

Edward remembered what the giants had told them about the accuracy of the girl's aim. The path had wound round the hill, and he ordered his men to step back a few paces, behind the safety of its slope.

Edward stuck his head out from behind the bend in the hill and again shouted at the top of his voice, "We have only come to rescue you! We mean you no harm!"

"I don't want to be rescued!" the girl shouted back.

She shot another arrow, which thumped into the hill just beside Edward's head. He knew that the next arrow would be aimed to kill.

The last arrow had been a surprise, but not nearly so much of a shock as the appearance of a grey wolf bounding down the side of the hill towards him. There was no time to string bows, so Edward and the other swordsman swiftly drew their weapons. The wolf came to a sudden halt halfway down the hill. It looked directly at the group of men before throwing back its head and letting forth a chilling howl. The wolf's cry would have made even the bravest of men shiver with fear, and Edward was no different. Not a man among them failed to feel his hackles rise or his skin turn to goose prickles.

However, instead of attacking, the wolf took a giant leap, taking cover behind a large boulder.

Bows were carefully strung, and arrows poised, ready to shoot the wolf if it reappeared.

"Harm my wolf, and I'll harm you!" This time, the voice came from above the place where the men were standing.

They looked up and saw a pile of small rocks start to move and tumble down the hill towards them. For a few fleeting moments, they caught sight of a young woman before she darted behind the boulder with the wolf. She was dressed in pieces of animal fur and had long, straggly, fair hair.

The men ran for their lives. They stopped after a few hundred yards and looked behind them. There was no sign of girl or wolf.

"She was warning us." Edward tried to stay calm and take back control. "The giants told us that she was deadly accurate with a bow and arrow. If she had wanted to kill me, or indeed any of us, she could have done so."

"Aye," agreed one of the older men. "If she hadn't shouted before she pushed the rocks down the hill, we wouldn't have had a chance."

"And then she hid behind the boulder with that wolf," another man added. "I've seen a few wolves in my time, but never one that wouldn't attack a girl if it had half a chance!" He shook his head in disbelief.

"Best leave her be," said one of the men, who was still trembling with fright.

"Yes," agreed Edward. "We will leave her for the time being, go back to the village, and report what has happened. Then we will decide what to do."

The men walked back a lot quicker than they had come, describing what each had seen and discussing their thoughts.

But Edward was quiet. He was thinking about the girl. He had caught a brief glimpse of her long blonde hair and pretty face. He remembered slender legs and arms, stretching out from the animal skins that hung from her body, as she leapt for cover behind the boulder.

When the party arrived back at the village, Edward told his father what had happened. Arthur looked questioningly at the other men who had been in Edward's party. They confirmed that the strange tale the boy had told was true.

"I think," said Edward, "we may have startled her because we were all men. Perhaps, if we had taken a few women or girls with us, she would not have been so alarmed."

"Hmm." Arthur considered his sons words. "You may well be right, but we cannot risk any more lives trying to speak to this girl. Anyway, it does not sound as if she needs to be rescued."

"I would like to try one more time," said Edward. "I have a plan, which I hope Gilda will help me with."

Edward gave his stepmother one of his winning smiles.

The witch furrowed her brow, wondering what favour he was going to ask of her.

Edward continued to tell his father his plan. "If Gilda would fly on her broomstick, up above the girl's cave and out of the range of her arrows, perhaps we could talk to her together. If Gilda would be kind enough to ask one of her fairy friends to come too," he added, giving his stepmother another charming smile, "the girl could see how beautiful the fairies are, and she would surely be enticed to speak with us."

Gilda, who was used to being persuaded by her stepson's charms, took his side. "Well, I would be willing to give it a try. It would be interesting to see this girl who talks to animals. She might even be a witch or part-witch."

Arthur was worried that his wife was putting herself in danger but agreed to let her go, providing she kept out of the range of arrows. Even if he hadn't agreed, Gilda would probably have gone anyway.

Despite a lengthy argument with his father, Edward was forbidden to go. His father spoke sternly. "I cannot put any of our men at risk, and there is much work to be done here. If that wolf attacked you, there is no way you could fight it off

40

on your own. If you ran away, it would soon catch you. A wolf can run much faster than any man."

Gilda sought the help of Elna, a young witch, and two fairy friends, Cherry Blossom and Franzipan.

However, Edward made sure he was close at hand when the four ladies met to plan their adventure. He still hoped that his father would relent and let him go too. The four friends decided to take the girl a bag of gifts. They planned to drop the gifts on the ground as they hovered above the cave; that way, they could quickly fly to safety if the girl fired an arrow at them.

"It will have to be things that won't break as the bag hits the ground," Elna said thoughtfully. "No good sending eggs or berries. Perhaps she would like some soap. I have some nice soap which I made last week, scented with roses."

"I have some violet essence she can have. I have preserved it in a very sturdy bottle which will not break. I have cast a spell of unbreakability upon it, and I can guarantee that it will not shatter when it is dropped." Cherry Blossom beamed with the pride of her achievement.

"I can make a spray of dried lavender which she can pin to her clothing," Franzipan offered.

"A brush and comb would be a nice gift," said Edward, who had been listening to the plans. "She has long hair which is a lovely shade of blonde, but it is badly tangled."

The women looked at him and passed knowing looks to each other.

"I am sure I can find a brush and comb somewhere." Gilda smiled.

Chapter 5 – Another Visit to Daisy

Edward's father and stepmother had told him most sternly that he was not to attempt to follow the four friends. He was trying to be adult about the situation, doing his best not to sulk. Nonetheless, he made sure he was there to see them off.

I'll put on my best face and not show my disappointment. I would far rather go with them and see that strange girl again instead of building dry stone walls, he thought.

Fairies cannot fly very far in one journey, because their wings are delicate, so Cherry Blossom rode with Gilda on her broom. Franzipan rode with the young witch Elna. The bag of gifts was tied to Gilda's broom.

They waved goodbye to Edward as they set off on their mission. Despite Edward's effort to put on his best face, the envy was apparent to the four friends. They all felt a little sorry for him.

It was fine day, if not a little cloudy, and a pleasant flight. Fairies never flew very high, and so they enjoyed the view below.

When they neared the top of the hill where the girl lived, they could see the opening to the cave. For anyone travelling up the hill, the entrance was concealed by shrubs, but the witches and fairies could see it as they looked down from above. The young girl came out and looked up, her wolf on one side and her goat on the other. A piebald pony grazed at the top of the hill where the land was flat.

"Greetings, young lady," called Gilda. "We bring you greetings and gifts from all who live in Merlport, the new village standing on the one where you once lived."

"What are you?" asked the girl. "I have never seen anyone riding in the air on a brush before!"

"I am Gilda. Elna and I are witches. We live with the people who dwell in the village now known as Merlport. Our little friends here are fairies who live nearby in the meadows round our village."

The fairies flew down and sat on some wild orchids a few yards away from the girl. They were afraid to go too close in case the wolf attacked them.

"Edward-Arthur, the boy you spoke to a few days ago, is my stepson. He and his companions meant you no harm. They are sorry that they alarmed you."

"They did not alarm me," the girl replied sharply. "I am happy as I am. I don't need other people. It was other people, called Trajaens, who murdered my family. How do I know that they will not try to harm me? How do I know that you are not trying to lure me back to the village so that you can make me into one of your slaves?"

"We do not have slaves in Merlport," Elna replied. "The very thought is abhorrent to us. No living being should be another man's slave."

The girl looked doubtful, but the fairies, in their tiny musical voices, confirmed what the witches were telling her.

"What is your name?" asked Gilda kindly.

"The giants call me Amazon, but my birth name was Daisy."

"Which name do you prefer?" Gilda dipped her broom nearer the girl, who made no attempt to string her bow.

"I was Daisy born and would like to be again."

"Well, Daisy Born, let us tell you about the people who live in the village."

Daisy listened while the witches and fairies told her about their journey to Avalon. She frowned when they told her that they had come in ships.

"The Trajaens came in boats," she said warily.

Gilda tried to assure her that the people who now lived in the village were not Trajaens, but settlers who would defend their land.

"You do not have to make up your mind now but please think about coming to live in the village. It must be a lonely life for you up here."

"I am not lonely! I have Billy, my goat; and Ruff, my wolf. I am happy here."

"Well, here are some gifts from our people," said Gilda, dropping the bag a few yards away from the girl so that she did not feel threatened. "I hope you like them."

"Thank you." Daisy gave a smile which lit up her pretty face. "You are very kind. I have listened to what you have said, and I will give it some thought." However, she was still wary as she watched the fairies fly back up to the broomsticks. "You really are beautiful creatures," she admitted as she watched the sunlight enhance the rainbow colours of their opaque wings.

Daisy waved goodbye. She watched the broomsticks and their passengers fly into the distance before picking up the bag and taking it inside her cave to examine the contents.

A few days later, the four friends flew back up to the cave to see the girl again. They were sure that this time Daisy would welcome the offer to join the people in the village. They even allowed Edward to follow them because, on their last visit, they had parted from the girl on such friendly terms that they did not feel the young man would be in any danger.

"Don't worry," Gilda had said to her husband before she left. "She has that wolf firmly under control, so it won't try to attack him; if it does, I will issue a stunning spell which will leave it unable to move for at least an hour."

Arthur had experienced Gilda's stunning spell once himself. He knew that her "speciality" spell, as she often referred to it, was very powerful.

It was a fine morning, with a light breeze blowing. Edward took the opportunity to push Challenger into a full gallop across the grasslands. He watched the two broomsticks soaring above him. The flyers preferred a gentler pace, especially since they had passengers on board.

The flyers breezed through a cloud above the cave at the same time as Edward neared the top of the hill.

One arrow after another shot up in the air as the broomsticks approached the cave. The witches were forced to steer themselves and their passengers up higher into the sky. An arrow whistled through the air, missing Elna's ear by just an inch.

"Go away!" shouted Daisy angrily. "Keep away from me, you evil people! Didn't you think that I would notice that lump of lard you gave me frothed like sea foam when I put it in my frying pan? Didn't you think that I would notice the funny smell of that cooking oil you gave me? You tried to poison me! Why can't you just leave me alone? I've done nothing to you!"

She shot more arrows in the air, even though she knew that the deadly points could not reach the witches, who were now too high to hear what she was saying.

"It wasn't lard; it was soap!" shouted Edward from the pathway, as he stuck his head out from behind the curve in the hill. "And the oil was violet oil, not cooking oil. You were supposed to wear it on your skin to make it feel soft and smell nice."

Daisy looked round, and when she saw Edward, she ordered her wolf to attack. Edward turned and ran.

Gilda swiftly dipped her broom, making poor Cherry Blossom hold on for dear life. The witch pulled her wand out from beneath her cloak and pointed it at the wolf bounding towards her stepson. As she uttered strange words, the wolf froze. It stood like a statue of an animal about to leap on its prey. Its lips were drawn back in a snarl, yellow teeth bared.

The young girl ran to the wolf and threw her arms round its neck. "What have you done to Ruff? You wicked people!"

Edward stopped and looked round.

Daisy stood, picked up a stone and threw it at him, but then turned back to the wolf, tears streaming down her face.

Edward ducked to miss the stone, and then stood tall again, watching the distressed young woman. He saw her drop her bow to the ground and throw her arms round the grey wolf again. "Ruff will be alright again soon," he called. "He will come back to life in a few hours."

Gilda was angry now. "Go. Go. Go. You foolish boy. Get away as fast as you can. It won't take her long to string that bow again, and when she does, her aim will kill you."

The two witches flew above Edward keeping watch over him until he safely reached the bottom of the hill. However, even as he reached his horse, Edward seemed reluctant to leave. He turned and looked back up the path, in two minds as to whether or not to turn back.

That poor girl. She doesn't realise that her wolf will soon come back to life. She looked heartbroken. I wish I could make her understand, he thought. However, the memory of the wolf's chilling howl and its bared fangs made the young man shiver.

Gilda shouted at him again. "Move, Edward! Move! Don't just stand there!"

Edward swung himself back into the saddle and urged Challenger into a trot. As he made his way back to the village, his mind was planning his next attempt to speak to Daisy. He just could not get out of his mind the picture of her looking so pitiful, holding the wolf and weeping into its fur. He just did not feel he could leave her. He wanted to make her understand that he was not the bad person she thought he was.

As the villagers saw the party returning, they gathered to hear the news. Everyone wanted to know whether young Daisy, the last of the Brewins, would be coming to live with them. They shook their heads with disbelief when Elna recounted what had happened.

Cherry Blossom's and Franzipan's faces were still white with terror.

"A fairy's wings could never have carried us as fast as an angry witch's broomstick," Franzipan stated.

Both fairies swore they would never travel on a broom again.

Gilda gave them some of Arthur's wine to revive them, and slowly the colour started to come back to their peachy cheeks.

"I don't want anyone else going up there again," said Arthur. "It is too dangerous, and I will not risk any more lives for the sake of one wild girl who seems perfectly able to look after herself."

All nodded their agreement, except Edward, who remained silent and thoughtful. Now was not the time to argue with his father, but he was determined to see Daisy again.

Edward remembered how soft her suntanned skin looked. Her hair was not so tangled, so he assumed she must have used the brush they had given her to comb her long, fair hair. He felt touched by the memory of the tears running down her face as she threw her arms round the ugly grey wolf. He remembered the tears he had shed for his mother when he found her lying in the river. He likened himself sitting beside his lifeless mother to Daisy hugging her immobile wolf, and shared her pain.

Just for a moment, Edward envied the wolf. How nice it must be to have someone throw her arms round you, and love you no matter how ugly you might be.

Chapter 6 – The Image of Greatog

During all the fuss about Daisy, Willy the Wood Wizard was hard at work. From the moment he started work on the trunk of the great beech tree, he seemed to have gone into a trance.

The old wizard had a small, triangular yard attached to his cottage, and it was here that he had gone to work. He had a wooden bench, and all his carpentry tools lay upon it.

Willy had removed his cloak and hat, and now wore only a thin cotton vest and boxer shorts. He looked very thin and old, but he set to work with the strength of a much younger man.

He worked feverishly, stopping only to drink water and swallow the occasional mouthful of soup, which his kindly neighbour had made for him. He hardly stopped, sleeping for just a few hours each night before resuming his task.

As he whittled away at the wood, beads of sweat ran down his wrinkled body and stained his vest. Villagers stopped to watch him, but if anyone spoke, he seemed not to hear them. As the days went by, Willy became noticeably thinner, and his craggy face turned a paler shade of grey.

In marked contrast to the hyperactive Willy, a very old wizard sat – or, rather, slept – in the corner of the triangular yard. He kept his arms folded and tucked inside his voluminous sleeves, and he had his hat pulled over his face. When he did wake up, he revealed a particularly kind face with a beaming smile.

For days and days, Willy maintained the incredible pace of work which no human could have managed.

King Arthur was worried, but the other wizards advised him to leave Willy to his work. They had seen him like this before and knew that he would not stop till he had finished.

While Willy worked, the men of Merlport continued to rehearse their battle skills. Arthur had ordered them down to the grasslands to practise archery. They had tried to practise in the village square, but the arrows which missed their targets proved to be too dangerous for those villagers going about their everyday business.

On their way to the grassland, they passed Willy, who was standing on a ladder, whittling away at the large tree trunk. They all stopped to stare. A few made humorous remarks.

Edward glared at those who joked about the little wizard. His stern face soon stopped the japes.

Edward strode over the rickety little fence which surrounded Willy's yard. He felt the need to ask the little wizard whether he was all right, but before he could reach Willy, Edward heard a voice.

"May I help you, young man?"

Edward turned to see the elderly wizard, who had been sleeping in the corner of the yard, standing at his elbow. He had no idea how the man had moved so quickly, especially when he had appeared to be very soundly asleep.

"I ...," Edward said hesitantly. "I am worried about Willy. He's been working frantically for days now. It is not humanly possible to keep working at that pace for such a long period of time."

"Ah," replied the other wizard, with a gentle smile that made his blue eyes twinkle. "But we are not human, are we?"

Edward shook his head. "No, I don't suppose you are. But," he added as he looked back at Willy, "he just looks so old and frail."

"In some ways, the older you are, the more resilient you are." The wizard beamed. "Willy is fine. He is always happiest when he is working. The harder he works, the happier he is.

Thank you for your concern, but please do not trouble yourself." The old wizard bowed his head as if to end the conversation.

Edward mumbled his goodbye, left the yard by striding over the fence again, and set off for archery practice. He looked round, to see that Willy's friend was back in his chair, hat pulled over his face, with all the appearance of being asleep.

The afternoon sun was hot. One of the witches brought some pale-coloured cream for the men to put on their faces to protect them from burning.

"What about Willy?" Edward asked the witch as he took some of the cream and smeared a thick dollop over his nose. "He will need some protection from the sun. His skin is so pale."

The witch smiled a toothless grin. "If Willy needs anything, his friend Tannitus will make sure it is provided."

"Who is Tannitus?" asked Edward.

"Why, his friend who watches over him. The gentleman who sits in the corner of his yard."

"But that gentleman spends his time sleeping!" exclaimed Edward. He then shook his head, remembering the unnatural speed with which the elderly wizard had appeared at his elbow earlier. Smiling at the witch, he conceded, "I am sure you are right."

The witch grinned and continued to offer her tray of soothing potions to the would-be archers.

Edward was still concerned about Willy. On his way back from the village, he stood to watch the little wizard labouring over the image of Greatog. A face and shoulders had been crafted, and the wood wizard was now working on the fingers of the folded arms.

"It's unbelievable, isn't it?" asked a familiar voice at Edward's side.

Edward looked down to see Connie. He had noticed her watching him several times as he practised his sword drill, even seeing her clap her hands each time his arrows hit the centre of the target.

"Yes, it is unbelievable," he said.

She smiled up at him. The same crinkly smile of which he had become so fond. Edward walked away.

"Bye, Con. Can't stop to talk. I need to get home and bathe. It was very hot out in the open today."

"I saw you. You hit the bullseye more often than anyone else," Connie called as she hurried after him.

However, Edward took his longest strides and quickened his pace. He really liked Connie, and it was because he liked her that he did not want to lead her on. His thoughts were now on another young woman, and he did not want to hurt Connie any more than he knew he was already about to do.

Connie realised that the young man who had become her heart's desire was now deliberately trying to avoid her. She felt deeply hurt. Tears stung her eyes and gradually trickled down her cheeks.

Day after day, Edward passed the wood wizard and stopped to watch. The speed and skill with which Willy used his various knives to carve the wooden image was incredible. But, as the days passed, the little wizard's body and vest looked dirtier and dirtier. His friend still continued to sleep in the corner of the yard, seemingly oblivious to Willy's worsening demeanour.

At last, the wood wizard ceased whittling away at the wooden statue, but still he did not stop working. He fetched the paints he had made, from flowers and plants, and set about painting the likeness he had created. Every now and again, Willy would step back and gaze at the likeness before carefully dabbing it with more paint.

Finally, he sat on the ground, exhausted, and just sat staring at the statue.

Almost simultaneously, Tannitus woke up and pushed the hat back from his face. The wizard asked one of the people watching to tell Arthur that Willy had finished his creation.

As soon as the king heard the news, he headed towards the triangular yard, limping as fast as his crippled legs would allow, to see the end result of the wood wizard's labours.

"It's amazing," said Arthur as he stared at the round face which Willy had carved. The face revealed a strong jawline with a mouth shut firmly, and a protruding nose. The head stood upon broad shoulders and folded muscular arms. The detailed carving stood upon a wooden, ornately decorated plinth. All had been carved in one solid piece from the trunk of the beech tree.

"But are you sure that this is what Greatog looked like? After all, you've never seen him. What's that funny little black lump underneath his eye?"

"The image you see is the image the tree gave to me. Nothing more, nothing less. You can leave the message for Zog, and you can see what he thinks when he gets here." Willy was not willing to discuss his work of art. "By the way, is Merlin back yet? I will need my broomstick again once I am rested."

The king told Willy that Merlin had not yet returned, but it was not unusual for the mighty sorcerer to be gone longer than he planned. He told Willy not to worry. He was sure that Merlin would return the broom soon, and in good condition.

One of Willy's wizard companions took a pink sock to the forest. He filled it with small stones and, as agreed with the giants, put it inside the hollow of the oak tree. The sock was carefully positioned, with a little bit sticking out of the hollow, to make sure that the giants saw it.

The next day, Zog and a band of giants marched down to the village. The villagers knew the giants were on their way before they saw them. The ground had already started to tremble with the weight of their heavy footsteps. Luckily, Willy lived on the edge of the village, so the giants did not have to venture too far into Merlport. The very stone walls of the newly built houses shook as giants passed.

When Zog saw the statue, he was delighted. "It's exactly like my father! You even put the black mole under his left eye! He hated that mole, but it was there, and it's a true likeness alright."

Arthur breathed a sigh of relief. He had not been convinced that Willy could carve a likeness of Greatog without ever having seen him.

The giants were invited to sit, take refreshment, and parley. Plate after plate of sandwiches, pies, and cakes were brought out to them. They ate and drank so heartily that the villagers were worried that they would run out of food and ale.

"So when will you make that old oak tree into a statue of me?" Zog asked.

"Let me rest for a while," said Willy. He looked strained and could hardly keep his eyes open.

"While we wait for Willy to rest, do you think we could select some trees to cut?" asked Arthur. "We really do need to strengthen our roofs with timber before winter sets in."

Zog nodded his agreement, and then he laughed. "I see you've been trying to talk to the girl we call Amazon. That young lad of yours is persistent, isn't he? We were watching the goings-on from the edge of our forest. She didn't make you very welcome."

"Well, a lot of it was a misunderstanding," admitted Gilda as she collected the empty plates. The giants had devoured a large quantity of home-made cakes and scones smeared with cream and strawberry jam.

Gilda continued. "I flew up there this morning to make sure her pet wolf was alright after the effect of my spell had worn off. After all, the wolf will protect her, and I wouldn't like to see her come to any harm. I see she's got a pet mountain lion now."

"Pet mountain lion?" asked one of the giants. "Are you sure?"

"Well, there was a mountain lion in the grass above the cave. I think it had injured its back because there was a long scratch which looked as if it had been bleeding. I couldn't see Daisy anywhere. The pony wasn't there either, so I assumed she had gone out for a ride," replied Gilda.

"That sounds like the lioness with the cubs." The giant looked concerned. "My brother had to kill the male on his way back from Twydell a few days ago. He'd been there to visit relatives, and the lion attacked him on the way back. He didn't like killing a lion, as there are only a few around. The lioness tried to have a go at him too, but he cut her with his sword. She ran away, with two hefty cubs at her side. Good job the cubs didn't join in; otherwise, it would have been my cousin lying dead instead of the lion."

"The lion wont attack when the wolf is there," said Zog. "But if it wanders away from the girl, she will have little chance against a hungry lioness with cubs to feed."

Young Edward was alarmed. He had sat in the parley with the giants but had kept quiet, listening intently while they discussed Daisy. Now he stood and faced his father. "We must go and warn her!" he shouted. "It wasn't her fault. She didn't know that the soap wasn't lard or that the violet scent wasn't cooking oil! We have to save her!"

"No," the king snapped. "I'll not put any of my people at risk for that girl again."

Father and son glared at each other and started to argue.

The giants looked at one another. Zog looked at his companions and winked. They had no wish to listen to the small people row with each other, so they politely said their goodbyes.

"Anyways, we will wish you good afternoon," said Zog loudly.

Arthur and Edward ceased their quarrelling – at least until the giants had taken their leave.

Zog continued, as if nothing had happened. "We'll take this magnificent statue of Greatog. Now, if Willy comes to the edge of the forest tomorrow to meet our forest master, I'm sure they'll come to some agreement about which trees can be cut."

Two of the giants lifted the heavy statue, and they all made their way back up the hill to the Great Forest, waving to the small folk and humming a merry tune as they went.

Chapter 7 – Lions

When the giants were out of earshot, Arthur and Edward turned on each other again. It was a rare sight for father and son to argue, and the ferocity of the argument was unprecedented. Wizzwits and humans alike stood back and watched, until Gilda intervened and put a halt to the argument.

"Edward is right, my love," she said gently to her husband. It was not often they disagreed, but her maternal instinct had come to the fore. "The boy is right. Daisy did not understand what the gifts were for. I've been thinking that we should go back and try to speak to her again. Now I know we must."

"Let me ride with you, Mother," Edward said.

"Two on a broomstick will slow me down." Gilda rushed off. "I must go."

Arthur sighed noisily. He knew that if his wife intended doing something, he could not stop her. However, he was determined that Edward would not risk his life again.

"Edward-Arthur, you come back here!" Arthur shouted as his son ran off after his stepmother. The king always used his son's full name when he was angry with him.

However, Edward was not going to be stopped by anyone – even his father. He mounted Challenger and urged the stallion into a gallop. He could see his stepmother soaring above him. When he got to the base of the hill, he dismounted and left his horse behind. He hurried up the path, panting heavily, but not stopping once to catch his breath. All he could think of was that Daisy might already have been mauled by the lion. She might be lying dead and lifeless, and he was too late to help – just as he had been too late to help his mother.

He could hear the agonising yelps of the wolf before he was anywhere near the cave. As he turned the bend, he could see the lioness on top of the wolf, her teeth sinking into its throat. Daisy lay pale and motionless, a few yards behind the wolf. The blood-drenched body of the dead goat lay beside her.

Edward's heart beat fast. *Am I too late?* He wondered as he reached for his bow.

Gilda dipped down on her broomstick, with her wand drawn. She issued the stunning curse just a second before her stepson released an arrow from his bow. The arrow hit the lioness in the chest and sank deep into her heart. The lioness was dead, but the stunning curse had left the ferocious beast lying rigid on top of the wolf.

Edward rushed to Daisy, who was now stirring and trying to sit upright. "Are you alright?" He put his arms round her, and for few moments, she sat rubbing her head and trying to focus her eyes. "I'm so glad you are still alive! I thought I was too late – again."

Daisy continued to just sit, leaning against Edward, waiting for her head to stop spinning. She tried to focus, and when she did, she saw her wolf still lying beneath the lioness. She pushed Edward away and forced herself to stand. She staggered towards the wolf, which was bleeding heavily and struggling to breathe underneath the weight of its foe. The wolf had suffered deep claw marks to his body, and the lioness's sharp teeth were still entrenched in its neck.

"Ruff! Ruff!" Daisy sobbed.

Gilda, who had been circling above to make sure that the lion cubs were not nearby and likely to attack, landed her broom. She and Edward helped Daisy lift the lioness from the wolf's body, but it was clear that the poor creature was dying.

Edward felt helpless.

The distraught Daisy tried to comfort Ruff, tenderly stroking his head as he breathed his last. "He was trying to save me. The lioness attacked Billy, my goat. I ran to help Billy, but the lioness turned on me. It was about to pounce when Ruff came between me and certain death. I fell back and hit my head."

Tears streamed from Daisy's eyes until they were puffed and swollen. The young girl sobbed so much so that her breath caught and her shoulders heaved. It was a long time before she stopped crying.

Gilda and Edward sat with her, trying to offer comfort.

"I must bury my pets," Daisy said. "I must get rid of this lion carcass before any scavengers see it. I don't want any thunderbirds smelling the blood."

"I'll help you," Edward volunteered.

"I will get help from the village," Gilda said. "You will need spades." Without any further hesitation, the witch flew off towards Merlport.

Daisy covered the dead animals with blankets. She and Edward walked to the top of the hill, where the ground was soft, and selected a place to bury the dead pets. Daisy was not sure what to do with the lioness. Edward thought she might want to make use of the animal's skin, but Daisy said that she would not want to wear anything that reminded her of the creature which had killed her pets.

"How did you know that the lioness was nearby?" she asked.

Edward told her about the giants' visit and that the male lion had been killed a few days before. He explained that the lioness had two growing cubs, and she'd probably been looking for enough food to feed all three of them.

"What?" Daisy said with a gasp. "You mean there are hungry lion cubs out there? We must find them, or they will starve!"

Edward was astonished.

Daisy forgot her grief and started following the tracks that the lioness had left. She followed the tracks back until she found the two hungry cubs hidden in the undergrowth. At first, they growled and bared their teeth, but Daisy spoke to them. She had a calming way with animals, and the cubs eventually allowed her to stroke them.

"I have some preserved meat in my cave," said Daisy. "I'll go back and fetch it. I'll set up a camp, here beside the cubs, until they trust me enough to come back to my cave."

Edward protested. "They are big cubs, Daisy, and will soon be able to fend for themselves. What if they attack you? They look pretty strong to me!"

Daisy laughed at him. It was the first time he had seen her laugh, and it brought a warm feeling to his heart.

"You must come back with us to the village." Edward tried to be firm with her. He was genuinely worried for her safety.

"No. I can't. I must stay here and look after the lion cubs. They will be my pets just like Ruff and Billy were. Ruff was just a pup when I found him. I trained him, and he eventually became my protector. These two cubs will take the place of Ruff and Billy, and then I will have two new protectors." The smile slipped away, and the sadness appeared in her face once more. "Although I am not sure that anything can actually replace my cuddly wolf or loving goat."

By the time Gilda returned from the village, a makeshift camp had been set up alongside the den in which the cubs were nestled. Gilda had flown above some volunteers from the village and guided them to the spot where the three dead animals lay. The men had brought spades, and they dug graves for Daisy's pets and the lioness. The bodies were carried up to the top of the hill and buried in the spot chosen by Daisy. She asked that the lioness be buried next to her pets. She had forgiven the lioness. She understood that the beast which had killed her pets was just a mother trying to feed her cubs in the only way she knew how.

The men grumbled that it was a waste of a good lion skin, let alone a wolf pelt. Edward hushed them and bid them not to speak of such things in front of Daisy. The men stayed no longer than was necessary. They lit oil lamps to guide their way down the spiralling path towards their horses. They hurried down the path and did not look forward to riding through the night to get back to their homes.

Edward insisted on staying with Daisy. The night had drawn in, and he was worried about her staying alone with the lion cubs without Ruff to protect her. Daisy did not want him to stay. She said that she had lived alone for a long time before she had Ruff, and he was just a little orphaned cub when she found him.

Edward was hurt by her rejection. However, Daisy was oblivious to the hurt she had caused him and adamant that she wanted to be alone to grieve for her pets.

"Well, if you insist on being alone, then so be it," he stated firmly, his face full of displeasure. He then added in a gentler tone, "I'm not going home, though. I'll sleep in your cave. If you get frightened, or just feel you need a bit of company, then all you have to do is call."

"Thank you, Edward." Daisy came towards him, stood on tiptoe, and surprised him with a kiss on the cheek.

The young man wanted to take her in his arms, but Daisy would have none of it.

Daisy didn't linger. She went straight back the cubs, kneeling beside them and stroking their fur. One of the cubs nuzzled up against her arm, just like a house cat.

Edward made his way back to the cave, using an oil lamp that Gilda had left for him. All the blankets had been taken, either to cover the dead animals or to use in Daisy's makeshift camp. There was straw on floor, and he pushed it together to make a soft place to lie, but he slept little. On a few occasions, he walked back up the hill to make sure that the girl who had stolen his heart was all right. Each time he checked, she looked snug, wrapped in the blankets, with the lion cubs curled up against her.

As he lay on the floor of the cave, the morning light eventually penetrated the entrance. Yesterday, he hadn't taken too much notice of the inside of the cave. Now he could see the herbs she had dried hanging from the ceiling and the smoked meat suspended above the fireplace she had made. On the floor were home-made baskets in which he could see dried fruit and nuts. Daisy was a remarkable young woman to manage alone here for so many years on her own. He had longed to hear her voice calling for him in the night, but Daisy had not found the need to rouse him. The young woman was self-sufficient and needed no one.

He found her where he had left her. Her eyes were still red from copious tears, and circled with dark rings. She obviously hadn't slept as well as he had thought. She must have heard his footsteps during the night and pretended to be asleep. But her bond with the lion cubs had grown stronger: one sat at her side, and the other on her lap.

She gave Edward a weak smile when she saw him. "Thank you for staying, but there was no need."

"Well, I'd better be on my way then." Edward was reluctant to leave, but it was clear that Daisy wanted to be on her own. He had come here without his father's permission, and he knew that the longer he stayed away, the angrier his father would be with him.

"You'll find some berries in the cave, and some nuts. Help yourself to anything you want to break your fast," Daisy called as he walked away.

Edward hoped that she still might follow him, but, sadly, the girl made no effort to do so.

Chapter 8 – Preparations for Winter

King Arthur forbade his son to visit the "wild girl", as he called Daisy, again. He was livid with his son for disobeying his order not to go with his stepmother. The way Arthur saw it, the boy had put his life at risk for one individual.

"One day you will be king of the people who live in Avalon. Look at me! I am no longer a healthy man. Soon our people will need a strong leader who is also wise. You may be physically strong, Edward-Arthur, but you are not wise. You cannot risk your life for the sake of one wild girl when you are responsible for so many others. There is no wisdom in helping one person when there are a hundred others here that need you. There are houses and barns to build before winter sets in. This is where you are needed, and this is where you must be!"

Edward knew his father was right. Reluctantly, he obeyed the order to remain in Merlport. However, Gilda found the time to visit Daisy on several occasions. She told Daisy that Edward had angered the king and been forbidden to visit her. The witch explained that the king was worried about his son's safety. As Prince of Avalon, Edward was expected to work alongside the villagers. He had a duty to make sure that there was sufficient food and shelter to see his people through the winter.

Daisy said she understood. She asked Gilda to give him a message thanking him for all he had done, and to tell him she was sorry for the trouble she had caused. She asked Gilda to tell him that the lion cubs were growing fast. They were living in the cave with her now but had just started hunting for themselves.

Gilda passed Daisy's messages to Edward. She added that Daisy was just like a young mother, running after the cubs when they went out in search of prey.

Edward longed to see Daisy but did not want to make his father angry again. Besides, he did not want people to think that he was shirking his responsibilities in Merlport. There were still a lot of preparations which had to be done before winter.

Willy had taken time to rest after finishing the statue of Greatog. A few days later, he had started work on the statue of Zog, going through the same process of working feverishly, in a trance-like state, while his sleeping friend kept watch. Zog had been as pleased with the likeness of his own image as he had been with that of his father. The giants had carried the statues back to their own village, and, under the supervision of Willy and their own forest master, allowed the Merlporters to cut more trees.

Merlin was still not back, so Arthur had a cart made for Willy to travel back and forth to the forest to select the trees for cutting.

When he was not travelling back and forth to the forest, Willy was resting. His hard work had taken its toll, and he needed time to recuperate. This was just as well because, otherwise, he might have wanted to use his broom.

"Have you heard from Merlin?" Willy asked Arthur as they sat watching Edward and the other boys sawing the tree trunks into timber roofing structures. "He promised he would be back with my broom in a week's time. It must be nearly three weeks now, and we still haven't heard from him. What's worse, he's still got my broom!"

"No, I haven't heard from him," replied the king. "But you know how unpredictable Merlin is. I'm sure he will show up soon, with enough stories about his adventures to fill a book."

The king tried to sound confident, but Merlin's failure to return was beginning to worry everyone.

Chapter 9 – The Battle of Merlport

Since learning about the marauding Trajaens, one of the Merlporters was posted at the top of the cliff, day and night, to act as a lookout. The lookout kept a loud horn beside him, which he would blow if he saw any approaching danger.

For weeks, the men took turns sitting on the cliff, but no peril was seen. Late summer turned into early autumn. One day, just as the new houses in Merlport were getting close to completion, longboats appeared on the horizon.

The bellow of the horn made one and all stop in the midst of what they were doing, turn, and look out to sea. Goose prickles rose on the skin of everyone.

The Merlporters had not come to this new land prepared for war. They thought that Avalon would be a land of peace. They prepared for battle as best they could. Those who had swords, or bows and arrows, picked up their weapons. Others, who might have been considered too old to fight, took up pitchforks and axes; they were joined by some of the women. Other women and children gathered baskets of stones to throw.

The makeshift army made its way to the beach.

The old women found rags and tore their petticoats into strips to make bandages, knowing that battle brought with it much bloodshed.

King Arthur donned his old armour, but it was now heavy on his aching shoulders. He took it off and told his son to wear it instead. He and Edward then mounted their horses and identified the positions that their men would try to hold. Eleven archers stood on the cliff-top; another sixty men stood on the beach, armed with swords, pitchforks, axes, and anything else they could use to fight with.

The women and children with stones knelt above the path leading up to the cliff. From that vantage point, they could throw stones when the Trajaens crossed the beach, as they surely would.

The witches, who were present in the village, sent messages on the wind to gather as many of their brethren and sisterhood as possible.

As the boats sailed closer into view, the villagers could see their foe. The boats were full of angry-looking, black-bearded men with brown skin, wielding swords and other spiteful weapons. They wore metal helmets with what looked like cow horns poking out on either side. The men on the boats were just as the giants had described the bloodthirsty Trajaens.

At last, the boats came close to the Merlport beach. As the Trajaens started to disembark, the witches and wizards dipped down on their broomsticks. With wands drawn, they each uttered their own special spells. Gilda issued a stunning spell which left one would-be marauder standing motionless half in and half out of a boat. Another cast a spell which melted the sword of a burly Trajaen.

A clever old witch called Azgoose created a cloud which rained pink goo over one of the boats. The Trajaens inside it found that their feet were stuck to the deck and their arms glued to their bodies, so that they could not use their weapons. Azgoose used her spell on another boat and shook her fist with glee as she saw the men inside struggling to move in the sticky substance which rained over them.

Arthur looked up and saw Bizzbuzz, a large, plump wizard flying overhead. He was so large, he needed a very sturdy broomstick which resembled a small tree trunk. Unfortunately, the weight of the broom meant that he could

not fly very high or very fast. "Bizzbuzz is going to get shot down by an arrow if he gets too close," he told his son.

However, Bizzbuzz stopped short of the enemy boats, and hovered. He drew a bag out of his coat. Holding up the bag to his lips, he appeared to speak into it. Out flew a swarm of insects.

"He's releasing his honeybees on the Trajaens!" Arthur realised. "I hope the insects don't get near our people. The last thing we want is to be stung by bees."

"No," replied Edward. "They're heading straight for the Trajaens. I don't think they are honeybees, though. Bizzbuzz wouldn't risk his precious bees. It's his wasps. Esmie said he was trying to develop a type of wasp that could make honey, but he's not been successful."

Bizzbuzz took another bag from his pocket, spoke to the contents, and then released even larger insects, which buzzed towards the Trajaens.

"He's been trying to breed honey-producing hornets as well." Edward laughed. "Unsuccessful at making honey, maybe, but his little pets seem to be doing a good job at assaulting the Trajaens, alright!"

The Trajaens tried to swat at the attacking wasps and hornets, and some of the raider suffered stings. Unfortunately, the insects seemed to be attracted to the pink goo. Many got stuck in the sticky substance, where they died.

Meanwhile, Azgoose was so pleased at the sight of a third raider boat inundated by the rain from her cloud of pink goo that she hopped aboard her broom and stood on it. She was an ugly old witch, so thin that she looked like skin over bone. Her nose was hooked, and her chin poked out and curved upward. The old hag made a bizarre spectacle of herself: she not only stood on her broom but actually started to dance. The Avalonians cheered the old woman on, but, alas, the triumphant witch was overconfident. Her foot slipped, and she tumbled head first into the sea. The Avalonians groaned to see their newly found heroine fall. Azgoose was last seen swimming out to sea, in an attempt to avoid Trajaen arrows. Meanwhile, her broom continued to fly along without her until it crashed into a cliff.

As the pink goo began to dry, the raiders were able to pick the goo, as well as the wasps and hornets stuck in it, off their bodies. Gradually, they were able to lift their feet from the decks of their boats. The pink goo had only caused a delay.

Willy the Wood Wizard was still without a broomstick. He took up a standing position halfway up the cliff. From this point, he threw disarming spells as far as his wand would allow. Many Trajaen swords fell to the ground before they could harm anyone.

Few magical people are able to cast a spell without a wand, and even fewer are strong enough to issue a killing spell. Now Willy's friend Tannitus, the very elderly wizard with the kind, smiling face and twinkling blue eyes, boarded his broom. No one had seen him fly before because he seemed to spend most of his time asleep. The old wizard did not need a wand. He dipped his broom till he could look into the eyes of his chosen victim, pointed a crooked finger at the victim's heart, and issued his spell. Five enemy warriors fell lifeless to the ground before Tannitus himself was brought down by a Trajaen axe. He, too, then lay dead in the shallow water, beside his victims.

As the enemy made their way out of the shallow water and onto the beach, Arthur gave the order for the archers to fire. Eleven archers poured their arrows down from the cliff-top, bringing several Trajaens to the ground.

About twenty witches and wizards had joined the battle, with others joining the fray when they heard the call on the wind. Queen Elvira hovered above her witches, shouting commands to her people and sending her own hexes at the enemy. It seemed as if an array of spells had been cast, almost in unison, sending one Trajaen after another into the sea.

However, the people of Merlport were still heavily outnumbered. There were at least ten longboats, each containing thirty murderous Trajaens. The odds stacked against the people of Avalon were high.

The men of Merlport rushed towards the Trajaens as they stepped out of the sea and onto the beach. Some of the Merlporters were on horseback, and others were on foot. Insults were thrown as metal clashed against metal.

Esmerelda was fearless. She uttered incantations and cast spells which issued green sparks from her wand. Each spell struck one of the would-be invaders dead.

Queen Elvira saw an arrow aimed at Esmerelda. The old witch pursed her lips to blow the arrow off course. The arrow shuddered and landed harmlessly against a rock. However, the old woman momentarily lost concentration as she watched her daughter veer her broom to safety, and was struck by an enemy spear. Elvira fell from her broom and plummeted to the ground.

King Arthur and his son sat on their horses, on the edge of the cliff, watching the fight. Edward was angry because he wanted to join the battle, but his father would not allow him.

"If you go to the battle and are slain, our people will give up hope," said Arthur.

"And if I do not join the battle, our people will call me a coward! Look! Our men are falling, and even Elvira, Queen of the Witches, has been brought down."

Edward felt helpless sitting above the battleground, watching people die, and he told his father so.

As the two argued, they did not see Trajaens climbing the cliff beneath them. The Trajaens had avoided the pathway, and the overhang of the cliff hid them from view. Three crept stealthily up on one side, and four more on the other. They knew that if the leaders fell, the Merlporters would give up hope and surrender to slavery.

A Trajaen with a large sword suddenly seemed to appear from nowhere, and he ran towards Edward. Another grabbed the reins of Arthur's horse and tried to pull him to the ground.

Edward raised his sword to deal with the Trajaen heading towards him. As he did so, he caught a glimpse of another emerging over the edge of the cliff, just a few feet behind the first. He knew he could not fight two burly warriors, and his heart sank as he saw a third rising up from the cliff.

As the prince's sword clashed with that of the first Trajaen, he heard a strange deep growl. He glanced sideways and saw a golden, partly grown lioness leaping at the second Trajaen and bringing him to the ground. Seeing a third Trajaen fall as he clambered up from the cliff, with an arrow in his chest, Edward knew that Daisy was close.

Edward could feel himself shaking, but he managed to bring his sword down on the first Trajaen. The man had also caught a glimpse of the lion, out of the corner of his eye, and quickly turned to see where it was. It was enough time to allow Edward to gain the advantage. A second blow rendered the attacker senseless, and he toppled off the precipice.

Just as the fourth Trajaen was pulling himself onto the top of the cliff, yet another arrow found its mark. At first, the man tried to pull the arrow from his neck, but it was stuck firm. His lifeless body slid back down the cliff.

The prince turned to see what had happened to his father. King Arthur, old and frail as he was, had managed to turn his horse, which had reared up and knocked his first attacker to the ground, unconscious. His second attacker lay struggling under the teeth and claws of the other partly grown lion, and the third lay dead, with an arrow in his back.

Edward was still shaking. He thought at first that it was fear because his heart was beating fast, but then he realised that it was not he who was trembling, but the ground beneath him. The giants were running through the village, waving menacing clubs and axes as they came. Down the hill they ran, towards the cliffs. They had always had the appearance of being big, clumsy men, but they descended the cliffs with an abundance of energy and agility.

The men of Merlport, and the magical beings, were heartened when they saw the giants coming to their aid. Just one swipe of a giant's club could render two or more Trajaens senseless.

The giants hated the Trajaens and were eager to get into the midst of the battle, sending enemy after enemy to the ground. They laughed heartily each time a Trajaen fell beneath their blows.

"I'm going into the fight!" Edward cried, ignoring his father's orders to stay where he was.

He looked to his left and saw Daisy taking her place alongside the Merlport archers. He felt proud of her.

Another witch, who could issue fire spells, had joined the battle. The Trajaens watched with dismay as they saw two of their boats burst into flames.

A horn sounded to the prince's right. It was a deep mellow sound which he did not recognise. The young warrior looked round, just before descending the cliff towards his first battle. He saw Merlin on a white horse, galloping across the meadow towards the beach. Merlin was followed by six soldiers, one of whom was blowing the horn. Another was carrying a standard, but Edward was too far away to see what the standard depicted.

The Trajaens looked startled when they heard the horn because they recognised its sound. They had not expected the vicious onslaught from the giants, who had never come out of the forest to protect the Brewins. Nor could they have expected the strange spells that left them disarmed, motionless, or covered in sticky pink goo. Now it seemed yet another threat was heading towards them.

Many Merlporters lay dead, more were dying or injured on the beach. However, as Edward entered the battle, his armour shining bright and his war cry loud and clear, all rallied round him.

Edward could see his friend Andrew lying on the ground, and hoped that the lad was only injured. The sight made the prince rage even more. Edward found a strength and fury he did not know he possessed. His sword felled Trajaens to his left and right, and he kept his blade at work.

Merlin was the first of his group to reach the cliff-top. The crystal hilt of his staff was glowing red. He pointed the hilt of his staff towards a party of well-armed Trajaens who were edging towards a group of Merlport farmers equipped only with pitchforks and scythes. Lightning streaked forth from the glowing staff, striking Trajaens in its fiery course, knocking them to the ground, lifeless.

As the soldiers who followed Merlin reached the cliff-top, the Trajaens saw the familiar standard of Twydell: three mountains above two green valleys. The Trajaens did not know that there were only six soldiers, because they could not see beyond the top of the cliff. They thought that that a whole regiment of trained Twydell soldiers had come to the aid of the Avalonians.

The Trajaens turned and ran back to their ships, leaving their dead and dying behind.

The giants ran after them. Although they did not like the feel of the salt water on their flesh, they ran into the sea. They chased the marauders as far as their height would allow in the depth of the water. Two giants caught a longboat by its tail, tipping it upwards so that the Trajaens within fell into the water. The Trajaens were unable to swim because their armour and metal adornments were too heavy, so they drowned.

The witch who issued the burning spells followed the boats out into the sea and managed to set one more alight, so that the boat, along with its passengers, sank into the deep ocean.

Edward looked towards his father. The look of triumph which had filled his face swiftly disappeared. The king had fallen from his horse. The prince turned and urged Challenger up the path towards the cliff-top; as he did so, he saw Daisy run towards his father.

"One of the Trajaens must have cut him with a sword before Leo reached him," she said. The young lion, whose shaggy main was now beginning to grow, sat proudly on top of the Trajaen he had felled.

"Don't worry about me," the king managed to say, though he spoke with difficulty. "I will live, but Gilda has fallen. You must find your stepmother, but even if she is dead, you must be strong. Act like a leader. Tell the men of Merlport that they have done well, and honour their dead. Thank the giants and the people of magic. Thank those strange soldiers who arrived with Merlin. Your people need you, Edward."

A woman with bandages rushed towards the king. Daisy was kneeling at the king's side, trying to stem the flow of blood from his leg with her hands. The older woman fell to her knees and tore the king's trousers, revealing a long, deep gash. Arthur winced with pain as she tightly wrapped the ugly gash with pieces of linen, but he pushed himself up on his elbow to speak.

Edward just stood and watched. He knew he should return to the beach with his people who had fought there, but he found it difficult to tear himself away from his father.

"Go, my son. Go, Edward-Arthur. Be the leader you will shortly be," the king commanded.

This time, Edward did as his father bid.

Edward found his stepmother lying on the beach, another witch and Cherry Blossom tending her. The fairies and elves had not joined the fight but had stayed close, ready to use their own special kind of magic to try to heal the wounded.

"She is alive, but badly injured," the witch said of Gilda. "She hit her head when she fell, and she is unconscious. We will take her back to the village, along with the other wounded."

"I will stay with her," Cherry Blossom told Edward. "You must go and do what you must do. I will find you if Gilda awakes." The fairy seemed to understand that the young prince had duties to attend to.

Edward thanked her and then set off to speak to each of the Merlporters who had taken part in the battle. He sympathised with those who had lost loved ones; he shed tears when he heard that Alex and Andrew, the two brothers who had been his friends, had died side by side. He praised those who had fought bravely and listened while they recounted their actions; he thanked the giants and the people of magic. Finally, he introduced himself to the small band of soldiers who had entered the battle last of all, alongside Merlin.

As evening approached, Edward felt exhausted. All the dead and wounded had been taken to the village, except the Trajaens. Elvira, Queen of the Witches, had been slain. Esmerelda, her daughter, wanted to execute the wounded Trajaens. Many of the other magical beings and humans agreed with her.

Edward tried to think what his father would do, and so took a different point of view. He argued that the prisoners should be put on their longboats, with enough drinking water to get them home, taking a message from Avalon. He said that the surviving Trajaens should tell their people that the Avalonians had been merciful on this occasion. They should make it clear to their people that the Avalonians were people of peace. However, if the Trajaens ever attacked Avalon again, they would be shown no more mercy.

Tannus, the son of the Tannitus, the elderly wizard who was able to perform the killing curse, challenged Edward. Tannus's father was dead, and the angry warlock wanted revenge.

"We should slay all the Trajaens and pile their bodies high in their boats," he argued. "We wizards and our sister witches can use our combined powers to blow their boats back from whence they came. Let their people know what will happen if they dare to come here again!"

Merlin supported Edward's plea for mercy. "I understand your anger," he told those who had lost loved ones. "Many of those who died were my friends. But if we slay the prisoners, we will then be as bloodthirsty as our attackers. Let them go home with a very clear message that we are a peaceful people, but strong, well organised, and able to defend ourselves."

"I agree," said the blacksmith's wife, whose two sons, Alex and Andrew, had been killed in the attack. Her face was full of pain, and tears ran down her face as she spoke. "Killing more of these savages will not bring my sons back. Send the marauders home in disgrace, with a message not to come back. If they do return, I'll take a sword and slay them myself!"

The Avalonians who wanted to execute the Trajaen prisoners knew it would be difficult to challenge Merlin and Edward. Now that the blacksmith's wife had stated her wish for leniency, those with opposing views reluctantly ceased to argue.

Although Tannus had begrudgingly stopped arguing to have the prisoners slain, he wanted to identify them in case any returned. "We should mark each of them so that, if any do return, we will recognise them and know that they have not learnt their lesson. They must understand that if they come back, they will pay with their lives."

All agreed to this proposal.

Tannus ran three fingers across each Trajaen's left cheek, leaving stripes like tattoos.

Merlin and Edward spoke to the prisoners before putting them on their boats, to find out more about them. The Trajaens told them that they were people of the ocean and had no fixed home. They thanked the Avalonians for their mercy and asked if they could take their dead so that they could be buried at sea. The Avalonians agreed; after all, they did not want the murderous Trajaens buried on their land.

The prisoners and the dead Trajaens were stripped of their weapons, their armour, and the gold and silver ornaments they wore. The survivors were carefully guarded, by armed Avalonians and Twydell soldiers, as they piled the bodies of their dead on to one of the longboats. The Trajaens pushed the boat containing the bodies of their dead warriors out to sea on the receding tide. They then clambered aboard the other remaining boats for their journey home. A group of witches stood on the beach and, puckering their lips, blew a wind which pushed the boats far out to sea. They watched the boats grow smaller as they sailed into the distance, until they gradually disappeared.

Chapter 10 – After the Battle

When Edward returned to the village, he found his father lying on a bed of straw in the village hall. His wife lay next to him. Daisy knelt beside Gilda, mopping the sweat from the witch's brow. The two lion cubs had curled up together nearby.

An exhausted Cherry Blossom had draped herself along the top of Gilda's pillow, and fallen asleep. Gilda had regained consciousness, waking from time to time but soon drifting back into a feverish sleep.

"They are doing all they can for her." The king looked sadly at his wife. "I thought my battle days were over." The cut at the top of his thigh was bandaged, but blood had seeped through, staining the cloth a deep shade of red. "I certainly never thought I would see my beloved Gilda in battle. She was magnificent, wasn't she?"

"She was indeed," agreed Edward.

"And you too, my dear!" The king spoke to Daisy this time. "I owe you and your pets my life."

"As do I." Edward looked tenderly at Daisy, who lifted her head to look at him. "I thank you with all my heart."

"I am so sorry I accused Gilda of trying to poison me." Daisy let her guilt pour out. "I was so foolish. I remember that my mother spoke of something called soap, which she thought to be a luxury. I should have realised that it was not lard because it smelt of flowers when I tried to cook with it."

"It was an easy mistake to make, Daisy. I'm sure Elna will make you some more."

"I still have some of the violet oil, though. I tried to smash the bottle. I threw it hard against the rocks many times, but it wouldn't break."

"Cherry Blossom put an unbreakability spell on it," explained Edward as he gazed at Daisy.

Cherry Blossom stirred when she heard her name mentioned, but simply smiled and fell back into her slumber.

"I rubbed some on my skin after I washed. Here, smell," said Daisy, offering Edward the crook of her arm.

Edward looked rather taken aback but did as he was bid. He took her hand and gently breathed in the scent of her skin. He noticed how soft and warm she felt.

"It's lovely," he said and then noticed his father watching them.

Embarrassed, he changed the subject. "Your lion cubs have grown. They are much bigger than last time I saw them. Obviously, you managed to train them, and train them well."

"I have named them after my parents, Leo and Sybil."

Daisy spent the rest of the evening amusing the king and the prince by telling them about the antics of the two lion cubs she had taken in. As night fell, she laid a blanket beside Gilda and lay down to sleep at the witch's side.

Edward offered to find her a bed, but she declined, saying that she wanted to stay close to her witch friend, in case she woke and needed help.

With a tinge of jealousy, the prince watched as the lion cubs curled up close to Daisy. He had no wish to leave his parents or Daisy, but he knew that he needed rest, as there was much to do in the morning. He decided not to go home to his bed, but, instead, fell asleep on a nearby pallet of straw.

Merlin had left Arthur to his family on the evening of the battle but was on his way to see him the follow morning when he spotted Willy. Willy was sitting on a stool outside his house. The elderly wood wizard had fallen against the cliff during the battle, and his arm was in a sling.

"Where is my broom?" Willy demanded.

"I'm sorry, old friend. It is broken and beyond repair. I will buy you another."

Merlin expected Willy to be cross and give him 'a piece of his mind'. However, the old wood wizard was still thinking of the events of the previous day, and he was melancholy.

"Never mind," he said. "I'm getting old now and don't really want to travel by broom any longer. The king has had a cart made for me to get backwards and forwards to the forest, did you know?"

"No," replied Merlin.

"Yesterday, it was used to bring back the dead and injured from the beach," he said sadly. "We thought that when we travelled to Avalon, we were coming to a new world full of peace."

"Yes," Merlin said with a sigh. "We lost old friends yesterday, but we have also made new ones." He tried to lift his friend's gloomy spirits. "I hear your images of Greatog and Zog were outstanding, and the giants came to our aid yesterday."

Willy pulled his lips, attempting a smile, but try as he did, his face remained cheerless. He simply looked more like a grizzled piece of bark than usual.

Merlin reminisced with his friend for a short while, but his errand remained, and he hurried away to the king.

"Where have you been for so long?" Arthur asked irritably as Merlin approached.

"It's a very long story, which I am eager to tell, but first I must give your response to an offer from King Frederrick of Twydell. The captain of the Twydell soldiers who escorted me home is to take your answer back to his king. He and his men are anxious to leave, as soon as their horses are ready. They all have families of their own and need to warn the Twydellers that the Trajaens have returned to our seas."

"Speak, then." Arthur was in pain but intrigued to hear the offer that the neighbouring king had made.

"Frederrick has a daughter called Jeanette and a son called Derrick. Both are of marriageable age. A marriage between Avalon and Twydell would form a powerful alliance."

Arthur understood. "It would indeed," he said thoughtfully, but he nodded towards where Edward and Daisy sat. They had spent much of the night watching over Gilda. Leo and Sybil curled up beside them, purring contentedly.

"I think Edward has already set his store with that girl. She saved both our lives. If he has fallen in love and wishes to marry her, I will give them my blessing. A loveless marriage to Princess Jeanette would not be fair to either of them and might also end up with a falling out with King Frederrick.

"Rosalie is still too young to be married. But if Derrick is willing to wait awhile, and they like each other when they meet, perhaps that would be a possibility."

"Very well." Merlin was disappointed, but he did not argue. He, too, could see the close bond that had developed between the young prince and Daisy. However, he added, "Derrick is a very affable young man. I think Rosalie will be impressed."

Merlin then hurried away to give Arthur's response to the captain of the Twydell soldiers.

The people of Avalon had fought a hard battle, and many had lost their lives in the process. Humans, wizards, and witches had fallen in the Battle of Merlport. However, the Avalonians had learnt much. They knew that they had neighbouring allies in the giants and the Twydellers. Most of all, they realised that the humans and the people of magic, together, were one people. Avalon was a peaceful nation, but the Avalonians would work together to protect their land from whatever dangers might come their way in the future.

More from the
Tales of Avalon Series

The Land of Twydell & the Dragon Egg, is the second book in the Tales of Avalon Series. It was published in 2016.

What happened during Merlin's trip to Twydell? Who, or what, did he meet? *The Land of Twydell and the Dragon Egg*, describes the wizard's extraordinary adventures in Avalon's neighbouring country and the people and creatures he meets there.

As he flies across the countryside on his broomstick he is puzzled to see a long line of people leaving the capital of Dalton and heading towards the outlying villages. Entire families are leaving the capital. They look ragged and downcast and appear to be taking their possessions with them. As he approaches Dalton, Merlin is shocked to see billowing smoke and that large parts of the city have been destroyed by fire.

The wizard learns that the devastation has been caused by a pair of dragons which have lived near the city for many years without any problem. King Frederrick is bewildered as to why the dragons should suddenly seek to attack the Twydellers for no apparent reason.

Merlin agrees to help the Twydellers and sets off on an unexpected adventure which brings him in contact with dragons and other strange creatures. He also renews his friendship with an old friend and is delighted to meet new ones.

If you like stories about magical beings then you will enjoy reading *The Land of Twydell & The Dragon Egg.*

The Exchange of Rings, is the third book in the *Tales of Avalon Series*. It was published in 2016.

The Exchange of Rings follows on from *The New Land* the first book in the series. It describes the preparations for the wedding of Princess Jeanette of Twydell to Prince Steven of Kerner. Rosalie is excited at the prospect of meeting Derrick, Prince of Twydell, who many hope will be her future husband. The weddings are an opportunity for each county to build new alliances.

Everything seems to be running smoothly but news is brought that wizards, who have been missing from Twydell's Forbidden Forest for many years, are being held in a Kerner prison. It is also revealed that fairies and elves have also been treated with cruelty by Kernans. The magical people of Avalon are furious and some want to take revenge on Kerner.

King Arthur of Avalon, Merlin the wizard, and their new found ally King Frederrick of Twydell, try to resolve the situation. They are concerned that revenge will be the beginning of war.

The allies hope that a solution can be found when the King of Kerner is forced to ask the magical people, of the Forbidden Forest, for help.

A Story Never to be Told, is the fourth book in the *Tales of Avalon* Series. It is to be published in 2017.

What happened to Azgoose, the clever old witch, who created the clouds of goo which delayed the Trajaens at the Battle of Merlport? Although the Avalonians sent out search parties, she was not found.

In *A Story Never to be Told* secrets continue to unfold. In this book we meet the Rabbart lll, the powerful King of Barrmin, and his family. King Rabbart rules all the former kingdoms and tribes in the northern lands.

King Rabbart befriends Arthur and the magical people of Avalon. He offers one of his beautiful daughters in marriage to Edward.

Is Rabbart lll's friendship with Avalon sincere? Will Edward remain loyal to Daisy, or will he marry a Princess of Barrmin to strengthen the alliance between the two countries?

The answers can only be found in *A Story Never to Be Told*

About the Author

Daisy Bourne was born in England, in 1917. Nothing much is known about her real parents, except that their lives were changed dramatically by the First World War. At the age of six, Daisy was unofficially adopted by a farmer and his wife. They changed her name and took her to Canada.

There are several similarities between the real Daisy Bourne and her namesake in this book. To a small child, Canada, with its heavy snowfalls, huge forests, and grizzly bears, must indeed have seemed like some kind of new

world. Although Daisy loved Canada and the farm on which she lived, she was not happy and ran away. She returned to England at the age of 16. In later life, she took up farming again. She also enjoyed her garden and preserving much of its produce. This is where the similarities between the real Daisy and the character in this book end.

I am proud to use my mother's birth name as a pseudonym when writing the *Tales of Avalon* series. My ambition is to one day write the story of the real Daisy Bourne. In the meantime, I shall work to complete the other seven books in the *Tales of Avalon* series.

A Note from the Author: I love hearing from readers, if you would like to contact me, please use the link on my website: www.TalesOfAvalon.co.uk or message me on my Facebook page: Tales of Avalon Series

If you enjoyed reading this book, why not recommend the Tales of Avalon series to your friends? But, please recommend them to start on Book 1 - right at the beginning of the tale so that they do not miss out on any of the adventures.

Printed in Poland
by Amazon Fulfillment
Poland Sp. z o.o., Wrocław

92321931R00068